CW00733691

All In The Game

Eleanor Hill

Published in 2000 by Onlywomen Press, Limited, *Radical Feminist Lesbian publishers,*
40 St Lawrence Terrace, London W10 5ST, England.

ISBN 0-906500-62-1

British Library / Cataloguing-in-Publication Data.
A Catalogue record for this book is available from the British Library.

Copyright © Eleanor Hill, 2000

Typeset by Chris Fayers Associates, Lower Soldon, Holsworthy, Devon.
Printed and bound in Great Britain by Mackays of Chatham plc.

This book is sold subject to the condition that it shall not, by trade or
otherwise, be lent, re-sold, hired out or otherwise circulated without the
publisher's prior written consent in any form of binding or cover other than
that in which it is published here and without a similar condition being
imposed on the subsequent purchaser.

Except for short passages for review purposes, no part of this publication
may be reproduced, stored in a retrieval system, or transmitted in any form,
or by any means, electronic, mechanical, photocopying, recording or
otherwise, without the prior written permission of Onlywomen Press, Ltd.

To my partner, Sue

Originally *All in The Game* was a story meant only for her.
But, in the way of such things the story grew.
This growth was greatly encouraged by
Rachel and Olive whose help with pruning
and shaping was invaluable.

1

She saw the ref look at her watch for the umpteenth time. "Come on, you bugger, blow your bloody whistle," she muttered under her breath. "Give us a break for once." Her throat aching, she moved back down the line and picked up the now cold thermos cup of coffee, draining it with a grimace. Boy, it was cold out here today, the November wind was really raw. The girls would be glad to get into the hot showers. "Good work, Penn," Robin shouted from the touchline as the central mid-fielder slid in for a vital tackle, whipping the ball from the toes of the opposition's centre forward. "Now, concentrate girls. Only three minutes to go. You can do it."

A few moments later, the ref blew for full-time. The final whistle brought a cheer from Robin. "You did it, you bloody brilliant bunch!" she yelled. "Next stop the final!" This was her team and they had played their hearts out today. The single goal had given them the break they needed, but they had held on to the advantage for a full hour, despite the intense pressure City had put them under. This new girl, Penn, was a real find. It was one of her unusually perceptive interceptions, followed by Carol getting a lucky bounce in front of the keeper, which had led to the goal.

Robin herded the team into the changing room, speaking to each one in turn. "That was an excellent save you made, Josie. Mandy, remind me about working on our free kicks next training session, you gave me an idea with that last one you took. Steph, you did well today but I know you can do better." Robin was a strict and demanding coach, but unstinting in her appreciation of a job well done. She knew the team appreciated her in return.

She noticed several of them shivering; some legs were blue with cold, not just bruises. "Into the showers all of you," she commanded, "and don't come out until you're properly warmed through. Steph and Carol, I want to see those bruises taken care of. Phil, how's the thigh holding up?" She continued on, attending to all the aches and pains, encouraging and bringing them all slowly back to the ground after their triumph.

Finally the players were clean, clothed and warm. Robin gathered them together again for the post-match post mortem. "OK. Listen up. That was an excellent result this afternoon and I know you're as pleased as me about it. But if you want to win the cup, and I assume you do?" She smiled broadly, knowing their desire for victory. "There's still plenty of room for improvement. First, defensively there were serious problems towards the end. Steph, you lost concentration every time you passed the halfway line. Their winger was past you and through on goal far too bloody often. You have to work on that. It's great how you support the attack but you have to remember you're playing defensive midfield, not centre forward!"

Steph shifted on the bench as the others chuckled. But Robin moved quickly on. "It's not just Steph, the rest of the midfield has to drop deeper to allow the forwards space to move. Carol, you've got to get in behind the defence down that wing, a few good crosses can make all the difference in a tight game. We've got to make more of our set plays, too. Castle Harriers, who we'll meet in the final, are a rough team. We're likely to have a lot of free kicks, and I want you to capitalise on them. Mandy's was a good effort today. We'll spend some time on that next week, so get your thinking caps on. We have to work on stamina too. You all look pretty knackered and the final could go to extra time, so you've got to be able to stay the course. But we'll get to that on Tuesday." The faces around her, although happy, were a little strained and Robin knew when to call it a day.

"I'm really proud of all of you," she finished up. "With more of this spirit, we may yet get some silverware in the cupboard." She waved her hand at the shelf over the door, empty as it had been for all four years of her time as coach with the Town. "And Penn," she added, "welcome to Deepdale Town, that was some game you played out there." The other players nodded their agreement, thumping the new member of the squad on the back as they made moves to leave. If Robin was giving particular praise, they were not going to hold back either. It was a rare event, but none of them begrudged the glow it brought to Penn's cheek.

"By the way, where d'you get the name?" It was Carol asking. Robin paused in the doorway, her curiosity aroused.

Penn flushed slightly. "My mum says it was in Pennsylvania that she got pregnant with me. On the honeymoon. My Dad was from there, so she thought this name would be special." She didn't add that her father had died only days after her birth. They would probably think she was soppy, and she wanted, needed, a tough image, here of all places.

"Well, I like it." That was Phil, the team captain, sealing the approval of Penn as a team member. She knew all about unusual names; she kept hers, Philomena, a closely guarded secret. "Now I knew a guy with a really weird name once ..." Robin, chuckling, left them to their gossip. It wasn't so long, after all, since she'd been that young and enthusiastic herself.

The team called their goodbyes to her as they left. "Bye," she called in reply. "See you all at seven prompt on Tuesday, you've still got work to do."

It had irritated Robin slightly when the women's training session was shifted at very short notice from the usual Wednesday slot. Tuesday left a longer gap before the Saturday match. But, after all, it was still the men who brought most of the money into the club. Deepdale was not one of the big clubs; it was a struggle to keep even the minimum of teams operating these days. The men had the first team squad, with their separate reserve team as back-up, and a smaller under-eighteen squad. There were probably about forty players on the permanent payroll, and another dozen who came and went more casually. On the women's side there was just the one squad of players, with numbers hovering around twenty.

Although Deepdale had a past to be proud of, in more recent years success had been hard to come by. This year, the men's team were struggling near the bottom of the second division, but Robin thought they'd survive in the end. She'd been a Deepdale Town supporter all her life and still thought of her job as something of a dream come true, unable quite to believe in it. The pay wasn't great but she made it up with her share in a local lesbian bar and nightclub, and it was good to feel she was part of the Town entourage.

What was even better was the fact that the women's game was gaining popularity with the spectators. It was making a real difference in all sorts of ways. The new deal over gate receipts meant a significant rise in funding for the women's game. It had been a real triumph when the national board had agreed to allocate all the receipts from women's games to the development of the women's teams, instead of diverting fifty percent to the men. Advertising and

TV coverage were beginning to pay serious attention to the higher levels of the women's competitions, too. This money was also staying in the women's game.

All this was excellent news for women's football, for the development of a full professional league. As yet, England's national professional league was small, just twelve teams, but it was resting at the top of a solid amateur structure. There were forty two teams in the three divisions of the national amateur league, and another hundred and twenty or so playing in lesser known, regional and local leagues below that. Each league had its own knock-out cup competition like the one Deepdale Town were involved in now, but the introduction of the All Leagues Cup a couple of years before had added greatly to the excitement of the season and begun to knit the women's game into a cohesive whole. Robin felt women's football was on the brink of the real breakthrough into the big time when it could match the men's game for attention. She did not question that the passion, flair and commitment already existed but the season needed to be extended, to fill the awkward gap around Christmas and New Year. At the moment it was like playing two seasons in one, she felt. The split structure was a result of the still primarily amateur status of the game, and the difficulties of travel, bad weather and poor pitches in the midwinter months. Plus many women found it harder than men to take time away from their families during the holiday period. With only twenty-six league games in a year, taking a break around Christmas had been the logical solution, but now, Robin thought, it was time things changed.

She'd played at all levels of the game herself. At one time she'd been the top scorer in Deepdale Town's women's team, but her career had been abruptly ended by a bad ankle fracture. As always when she recalled the incident, Robin's hand strayed down to the old ache in her left ankle and absently massaged the joint. She'd thought the world had come to an end when the physio told her she had no future as a player. Coaching seemed a very poor alternative in those early days. Robin smiled to herself as she thought back to her first triumph as a coach with the junior team. Even after all these years, the recollection brought a sweet pleasure. There was far more than she'd realised to the tactical side of the game, and developing this understanding to complement the players' existing technical skills brought her intense satisfaction. In many ways, the players growth in confidence on the pitch seemed to be mirrored in their lives outside football, she reflected. Her own passion for the game fuelled the commitment she felt.

"And god knows, some of these youngsters need all the support they can get!" she muttered to herself, knowing many had few other options or resources. "Still, this looks like being the best year yet. I've got the makings of an excellent team here." She locked up the office and made her way out of the ground.

As always, she paused in the car park and looked up towards the great humpbacks of the dales. A last burst of sunlight caught the jagged lines of the dry-stone walls, as the clouds chased across the steep hillsides in an ever-changing pattern of light and shade. She'd lived within sight of these hills all her life and could not imagine a world without them. From the dull browns of winter through to the lush green and gold of summer, the hills formed the backdrop to her life. The layered rise and fall of their slopes was as familiar as her own breathing. She sighed, wishing she had time to drive into their welcoming depths, but it would be dark in no time. She got into the car and moved off smoothly.

2

It was getting on for eleven, Robin realised, a little surprised as she checked her watch. The long, low room was packed, every table was crowded, women lined the walls and stood two or three deep along the bar. The wood-panelled walls emphasised the dimness of the lighting behind the bar, throwing the small stage area into sharp contrast. The act tonight had been a popular local singer, so the turnout was better than usual. Loretta could blast out a song with the best of them but tonight she'd done a full set of throaty blues, her intensity captivating the audience. The room had fallen quiet for several moments after her last number, but now she was surrounded by a sea of admiring women who clamoured for her attention as she manoeuvred through them. The takings would be good, Robin thought with satisfaction. She saw Sally moving towards her through the throng of women scrambling to beat the cry of "last orders" at the bar.

She'd known Sally since childhood, counting her among a small band of intimate friends, and they had set up the bar together five years ago, after Robin's injury. It was funny how things worked out. During their childhood it was Robin, junior by four years, who took charge. She led the way into a variety of adventures, persuading a reluctant Sally to be her accomplice. The nearest they came to serious trouble was during a night-time chase through a building site when Robin ran full tilt into a scaffolding bar and knocked herself out. Sally had patched her up, even back then. She knew Sally had not understood her exhilaration, brought on by the smell of cement, brick dust and damp scaffolding boards and the thrill of being in a forbidden place. Yet in adulthood, Sally was the one to push for a little risk-taking here and there.

The opportunity to buy the bar had arisen while Robin still had her ankle in plaster. Sally had neither cash nor property but persuaded Robin to raise the funds using her house as security. There'd been a lot of renovation work to do and it had taken a while to build up their reputation and clientele, but she'd never regretted the decision.

"This should help with the Christmas fund," Sally said happily, giving Robin a wink. Sally was a small round woman, with a frizz of mid-brown curls and soft brown eyes. She had a tendency to worry about everyone else's welfare. Other than that, she was level-headed and had a mischievous sense of humour. Sally had been with her partner, Ingrid, since their teens, and the two of them appeared to be a permanent fixture. Ingrid was thin with ash-blonde hair lying close against her skull. The impression of stillness she gave was deceptive, and her methodical manner was coupled with a dry wit. Calm, solid and dependable, she'd quickly become the anchor point of Sally's world.

Robin on the other hand had not come anywhere near settling down, as her mother would have said. This was not for lack of opportunity. Robin was never short of lovers. She was a striking woman at five feet ten in her bare feet, with an androgynous figure. Her hair was dark with a touch of silver, having a style of its own, rather than one Robin gave it. After the general impression of energy she gave, it was her eyes one noticed. These were surprisingly direct and clear, mother-of-pearl grey in colour with a darker rim to the iris. The laughter lines only added to their attractive power. Her face was angular, her mouth wide with an upward curve at the corners as though she was always on the verge of a smile. The only hint of vulnerability was in the hollow of her throat, just where the collar-bones met. It was a spot to which many women had felt tempted to put their lips.

"Mary not in tonight?" Sally asked, referring to Robin's latest girlfriend. Robin shrugged "I think she said she'd be by later."

"Oh oh!" Sally laughed. "It's reached the boredom stage again has it, love? You do get through them at a rate, don't you?" She smiled to take the sting from the words.

"I think she may have found someone a bit more on her level," Robin answered. "Oh, alright, I admit it. The pleasure is wearing a bit thin." She grinned at Sally's nod of confirmation.

Sally was always first to notice when a new woman caught Robin's roving eye, teasing her mercilessly about cradle-snatching. Robin had tried to explain the attraction. "They're always so eager, so fresh. The world hasn't worn them down yet, they're fun and don't get all serious on me. Besides I get enough of older women with you and Ingrid!"

"Not to mention how much they're flattered by your attention!", Sally teased. "But how do you keep up with them? It's all late night discos and parties with youngsters. I like our nights in, with the curtains drawn and the TV on. You'll burn yourself out before you're thirty."

"That leaves me with a few more months at least, before I join you two and your zimmer frames! I better make the most of it." Robin laughed, but admitted "they can get a bit exhausting, after a while, all that emotional intensity, worrying about broken friendships, always nagging at me to talk to them, really talk, you know, m·e·a·n·i·n·g·f·u·l." She drew out the word into an exasperated sigh.

Sally chided her, "That's what lovers do, you know, they talk, they share, they even get to know each other's secrets. It's not to do with age, it's part of the process of falling in love."

"So you keep telling me, but I can't stand it. It suffocates me, someone always wanting to know my thoughts every waking moment." Robin grimaced. "What's so wrong with wanting to have time to myself now and then?" Mary had been with her for five weeks and the dreaded 'meaningful' refrain had begun to creep into their conversations. Robin thought it was about time she moved on.

Sally knew her friend well enough not to mention wanting to have your cake and eat it too, and let the conversation drop.

Mary did indeed come by later, dashing in through the doors in her customary breathless fashion just seconds before closing time. She paused just inside the doorway smoothing her unruly auburn hair as she caught her breath. With one quick glance round the bar she located Robin, skipped across the room and hugged her. "Sorry, I couldn't get away earlier," she said softly, frowning as she felt Robin withdraw slightly from her embrace. She was an effervescent young woman, her body and face always animated. Now, her excitement ebbed and was replaced by a look of hurt reproach. "You know I have to stay to the end," she pouted. "That's when the lighting gets really complicated." Mary was a trainee theatre technician who harboured an ambition to cross over to the other side of the stage lights. She was currently on work experience, in the final year of her course at the local college. This meant that she was younger than usual, even by Robin's standards. Just twenty.

"It's OK." Robin relented slightly. "Are you hungry? Then let's get something to take home," she finished at Mary's nod. They called goodbye to Sally and went out to the car park, where Robin's dark green, second hand car waited. She loved it as if it were a Jaguar, her lifeline, promising freedom and distance.

Picking up a take-away, Robin drove home. She lived in a prosperous leafy suburb where the majority of the residents had what the popular press called alternative lifestyles. This suited Robin perfectly as nobody bothered her and there was no pressure to become neighbourly. She'd spent many happy summers in the house as a youngster while the aunt who had left it to her was still alive. It was a large rambling house with a wilderness garden which Robin kept that way through skilful but barely detectable control. Inside, the house was more an uncontrolled wilderness; while Robin might have heard that cleanliness was next to godliness, she knew for certain housework was the invention of the devil.

"Get some plates, would you?" she requested of Mary, "and let's take these up to bed." Suddenly she felt hungry for more than just fried chicken. She patted Mary's behind softly as she came back with the plates. "I'm hungry," she murmured with a glint in her eyes. Mary responded with a slow smile, flicking her tongue over her lips.

They ate the chicken quickly. Then, while their fingers were still dripping with the chicken juices, Robin began to lick Mary's hands, moving her tongue slowly, trailing up the inside of one arm, finally claiming her mouth in a long kiss. Her hands moved swiftly to remove Mary's clothing, revealing the warm freckled skin beneath. Robin's breathing quickened. Mary's head dropped back inviting Robin to kiss her neck. Slowly, she trailed her lips downwards, lowering her mouth onto Mary's nipple, suckling and nuzzling, relishing the textures in her mouth. Mary pulled her closer, her fingers working Robin's jeans loose. She slid her hands under the denim. Robin rolled, changing their position so that Mary was astride her. She held Mary still, savouring the moment, watching the quivering breasts and stomach. Mary lowered her hips, and Robin held her breath as she felt the moistness on her belly. She pushed against Mary's weight, straining to bring her closer. Her fingers moved surely into Mary's warmth, spreading her, thrusting upward. Mary rode her hand with gathering speed. Her orgasm, when it came, caused her to gasp with pleasure and Robin felt her own body contract in response, revelling in the release it brought.

"Oh Robin," Mary murmured, already half asleep. "You make me want you so much." Robin, holding her, smiled into the tangled curls still caught around her shoulder. "Go to sleep now," she said. "It's late and I have to be up early in the morning."

3

Robin woke before the alarm and got quietly out of bed, leaving Mary asleep. She loved the early mornings, before the rest of the world really woke up. Often she would run at this time, just a few miles. Her usual route took her up through the tree-lined suburban neighbourhood, which straggled onto the moor's lower slopes and along a little-used back lane. This was her favourite part of the run. On her right the moors stretched upward, a riotous surf of bracken, heather and tall feathered grasses which swayed and whispered in the wind, never still, brushing right up against the low stone walls of the lower slopes. This expanse was broken at irregular intervals by bulwarks of stone standing sentinel against wind, rain and vegetation. Their worn and twisted shapes testified to the cost of such intransigence. Occasionally Robin saw a kestrel or, more rarely, heard the lonely call of a curlew in the distance. To the left was Deepdale itself, nestled into the junction of three valleys. The grey stone of its buildings rose up the valley sides, mirroring the rock outcrops high on the surrounding moors.

From the hillside, she could see the whole of the town. In the centre was a small open market flanked by a railway station, the town hall and the public library. All of these dated from Victorian times when Deepdale prospered with the expansion of the railways. These central buildings were about four or five miles from where Robin was running on the town's northern outskirts. In between was a mixture of well-spaced semi-detached houses such as the one she lived in and smaller, more crowded terraces. Deepdale stretched for a similar distance up the other two valleys. To the west, lining the railway and motorway link road, were the small mills and warehouses now home to a variety of light industries and mixed in with a range of more modern buildings. Only the occasional patch of residential housing still survived here, and the football ground was easily spotted, a green space amidst the dark sprawl. The expansion of Deepdale to the southeast was the most recent, and in Robin's eyes the least attractive, consisting of two or three large, soulless housing developments. Robin returned from her run coming down off the heights through some lovingly restored terraced houses. Her ankle could not take long runs, but she still enjoyed the shorter ones and took pride in maintaining a high level of fitness. She completed her workout with stretches and push-ups.

She was already showered and dressed, fixing some shelving in one of the spare rooms, when Mary finally woke. "Hi there, sleepy-head," she called as she heard Mary pass on her way to the kitchen. "There's bread in the bin. Or would you like a cooked breakfast this morning?" She had discovered that Mary's morning appetite could be considerable.

Robin put her tools to one side and went down only to find her younger companion staring vacantly out the window. "What's up?" she enquired, her heart sinking as Mary turned her face and she saw the pout of her lips. "*Oh shit*," she thought. "*Here it comes.*"

"Why don't you ever stay in bed in the mornings any more?" Mary's tone was petulant. "You used to make love to me in the mornings. You know I want you then." It was more an accusation than a statement of desire.

Robin hedged, trying to avoid the honest answer. "I've been busy with a lot of things around the house," she offered, knowing it was not enough. She had a feeling this was going to be a final argument.

"And you've never let me touch you inside. If you really cared, you'd want me to touch you." This time there was a catch in Mary's voice, and, briefly, Robin felt a pang of guilt.

"You know that's not your fault," she countered, "it's just how I am. I prefer not."

"It's not fair! Why don't you want me to? I wouldn't hurt you." Mary's tone, like her expression became eager. "I know what to do ... Hilary showed me ..." And then she stopped, horror appearing on her face. "I mean ..." she stammered. Tears sprang to her eyes, spilling over down her cheeks. Robin moved to hold her, knowing an easy way out was found, her own failings no longer the issue.

"It's OK," she said, "you knew this was never going to be a permanent arrangement, didn't you?" Her tone changed, becoming lightly teasing. "Who's Hilary? I hope she appreciates you the way you deserve." She steadied Mary with a quick hug. "Come on, dry your eyes. It's not the end of the world."

Mary raised a tear-streaked face to hers. "I do care for you, Robin. I didn't mean for this to happen. It's just that Hilary ... well, she and I ..."

Robin persuaded her into a chair. "I believe you," she reassured Mary. "It's just that you and Hilary get on so well, and you didn't realise what was happening, hey?" She gave Mary a chance to get out with her pride intact, listening calmly as she explained the unknown Hilary's charms, describing a woman who, it seemed, looked very much like Robin. She did not let Mary see her amusement. "She sounds like a really nice person," she managed to say, convincingly enough, at the end of the tale.

"You better get on back home," she said to Mary, when they seemed finally to have run out of words.

Uncertainty returned to Mary's mobile features for a moment. "You'll be alright, won't you?"

"Sure, I'll be fine." Robin said lightly. "No hard feelings, sweetheart. You'll let me know how things turn out, huh?" She breathed a sigh of pure relief as she finally got Mary out of the house, and safely out of her life. It hadn't been as bad as she'd feared. Mary would be alright, too.

She returned to her shelving and was soon absorbed in the task. As she worked, she reflected on Mary and the other women who had passed through her house and her hands. It was a familiar pattern by now, and briefly she wondered if she was going to repeat it forever. It wasn't exactly an enthralling prospect. *"You'll meet somebody, someday, who'll be different,"* she told herself. *"It's just a matter of time."* She sighed heavily, and then shrugging her shoulders as if to shift a weight, went on sanding the wooden shelves.

<u>**4**</u>

The bright March sunshine blinded Robin as she struggled to see across to the far side of the field, the wind whipping her dark hair around her face. "Shape up, you lot! Come on! Let's have a bit of concentration in there!" What was wrong with the team today? Most of them seemed to be half asleep. The Town were lucky not to be five down, she thought bitterly, instead of just two. It was only Josie in the goal who was playing at anything like the usual standard Robin set for her team.

The dressing room was quiet after the match. She let them stew in the atmosphere for a few moments. It was their second loss in as many matches. She could feel their shock. Since winning the cup in January, they had enjoyed a run of four games without defeat, but it was well and truly over now.

"Right." She had all their eyes immediately. The group knew that tone of voice, even if they hadn't heard it for a while. They braced themselves for what was to come. Having enumerated in some detail just where they went wrong over the preceding ninety minutes and berated them for a bunch of half-hearted amateurs, Robin finished by asking of no one in particular, "So. Who can tell me the explanation for such a shambles?" Receiving no reply and realising that even Phil was looking glum, she made a deliberate effort to lighten her tone. "*Steady on, girl,*" she told herself. "*Don't overdo it.*" Out loud she quipped "The only explanation I can come up with is an outbreak of spring fever - so out with it ... Who's in love with who?"

"Come on, Robin." Phil, ever trustworthy, rallied to her attempt at humour. "You know we're all in love with you." At last, the atmosphere lifted as the team collapsed into laughter. Robin made no secret of her sexuality with this bunch, but she was careful to keep the flirtations light and general. Sex and coaching did not mix; she took the latter too seriously. She'd seen one or two of the team in the bar, and knew there were several lesbians among them.

"Well then, for my sake, let's do better next time, huh." She put her hand to her heart in exaggerated pleading. "You're the same team that won the cup just a few weeks ago. Remember that when we play Rangers on Wednesday night. I want to see your heads held high. You know I don't ask for anything but one hundred percent effort. As long as I get that I'll be happy. You don't always have to win." This last comment drew wide grins from the longer serving members of the squad. They knew she wanted to win more than any of them. The rivalry with nearby Hollowdale Rangers was an especially intense one.

At the training session on Tuesday, Robin was pleased to see the squad in much better form. They were passing well and thinking ahead of the game. Tomorrow might not be another disaster after all. Her only remaining concern was Penn, who was still looking out of sorts. She seemed unable to concentrate, making several silly mistakes, and Robin was worried to see the confidence draining away from her limbs. It was vital that this talented player stay on top of her game. During one of the rest periods, she checked quietly with Phil who had no explanation to offer, her open brown features showing her concern. "She keeps any worries pretty much to herself, Robin. I haven't been able to get anything out of her."

Robin nodded "OK. Thanks anyway. I appreciate your help." She gripped Phil's shoulder with affection and moved on. Phil was a good captain and usually managed to draw out the other members of the team if something was bothering them. Penn must be a tough little nut, Robin mused, if she'd resisted the captain's enquiries.

She passed through the changing rooms as the players were packing up to leave. "Penn. Can you give me a moment in my office." She made it an order not a request.

"Yes, Coach. Be right there." Penn was the only one of the team who persisted in using her formal title, all the others called her by name. Robin found it mildly irritating, but it was always said with respect so she decided to let it ride for now.

Robin had decided on a little positive inducement; she had the feeling that encouragement was more likely to produce results. Penn seemed pretty hard on herself. She was trying not to show it, but her face betrayed her when she entered the office a few minutes later. She thought she was in for some rough words.

On the field, Penn Millard appeared of considerable size but in fact she was a slight girl, only about five foot four. Her body was slim, in a muscular and rounded way, with small but firm breasts, an aspect she would have happily done away with as unnecessary. She had a thatch of blond hair which she kept cut short, never more than a couple of inches in length. Her brows were strong and straight across her forehead, drawing a line above her deep-set blue eyes. Her features were completed by an up-tilted nose, a determined chin and dimples either side of a sensuous, full mouth. She looked considerably younger than her twenty three years.

"Sit down, Penn." Robin motioned her to the bench. "There's a trial coming up in a couple of weeks," she continued, noticing the puzzlement which briefly crossed Penn's features. No, this wasn't what the kid expected and she had her interest now. "It's being organised by the top league teams in the region. It's an annual event, I don't know if you've heard about it?"

Penn shook her head. "Well, it's not an open event. Players have to be nominated. They form up seven-a-side teams on the day and run a knock-out competition. There'll be three training places up for grabs at the end of the day." She turned and looked directly at Penn, still concerned by the dejection evident in her posture.

"I'd like to put you in for it. Are you interested?" Penn's eyes grew wide and her face lightened, coming the closest to a smile Robin had seen her manage in several days.

"Yes, Coach," she confirmed, "I'm interested alright. But," she hesitated briefly, "there'd be others should get the chance before me." As usual, Robin was surprised by Penn's diffidence off the pitch. Despite her obvious talent, she never pushed her claim over longer established team members.

She squatted down in front of Penn, bringing their eyes level. "True," she agreed, "but I think you're the one with the real chance to make it to the top. The next chance won't be till next season and I don't think you should wait that long. I know the others'll understand. They believe in you, Penn. We all do." She gave Penn's knee a strong squeeze and stood, moving away so that Penn would not realise she'd seen the blush coming up under her skin at the compliment.

"But why now? I've been playing lousy and you know it."

"Yes. I was coming to that." Robin's voice grew sombre. "Can you tell me what you think the problem is? Then maybe we can work on it together." She faced Penn again. The young woman opposite her was bent forward, her head held in her hands, misery in every line of her body.

Robin moved quickly to her side "Penn, my dear, what on earth is the matter?" Her arms went around the slight form as Penn turned her face into Robin's chest, sobs breaking harshly from her. "It's OK, it's alright. Let it all out now."

Robin's concern was genuine, as it would have been for any of the team in such circumstances. She rocked Penn slowly back and forth, letting the storm of tears blow itself out, before pulling a tissue from her tracksuit pocket.

"I'm sorry." Penn apologised, hiccoughing, and then blew her nose with some force.

"No problem." Robin said. "Can you tell me about it?" She moved back slightly, but kept eye contact. Penn drew a shaky breath and nodded her head.

"It's my stepdad," she began. "I mean he's the one made me leave. He was trying it on, and I wouldn't let him." Her eyes dropped from Robin's concerned gaze, full of embarrassment. "He's been doing it for years, but Mum can't see it." There was desperation in the young voice. Robin seethed: just one man's uncontrolled craving for sex and power and such a devastating effect. Here was Penn, the most talented youngster she'd seen in years, her skills crumbling away with her confidence. Robin's helplessness only doubled her anger.

The rest of Penn's story followed, haltingly told. It was not such a rare one after all, Robin thought angrily. Her mother had married again when she was seven. At first all had been well, but when Penn hit puberty the problems began. She tried never to be alone with her stepfather, but after the recent move to Deepdale she had found it harder to make excuses to stay out of the house. In addition, her mother had gone on the night shift. Penn had spent as much time with friends as possible but had to go home sometime. He'd attacked her, and she'd only just managed to escape, blacking his eye in the process. An almighty row with her mother had followed, when she tried to tell her what was going on. Penn had left the house with her mother's condemnation sounding in her ears. She couldn't go back. He would be there, waiting, knowing her mother did not believe her. And she was damned if she'd give him any satisfaction. Penn had her pride and was stubborn with it. Giving in was plain impossible, she was determined about that.

"Where've you been staying, then?" It was a struggle for Robin to keep her voice from shaking. She felt very protective of her team members, and Penn, with her apparent youth and innocence brought this out strongly.

"In a B & B," Penn replied, "but I've not got much money, and I haven't been able to find a job yet to earn more." The note of desperation crept back into her voice, and Robin thought quickly.

"Well, that's one thing I can help you with then," she said firmly. "I've got spare rooms a-plenty in my house, and if you can cope with my company, you're welcome there until we sort something better out. OK?"

"I can pay," Penn began, but Robin cut her off quickly.

"Don't be ridiculous, girl. I don't need your money. Save it for other things. As I said, the space is there; it's no burden to me." Penn, utterly exhausted, submitted meekly after some further protest.

Robin drove away from the ground following Penn's directions to reach the small B & B. It was out to the western side of Deepdale, tucked into a small triangle of scrubby wasteland trapped between the railway line, some half derelict warehouses and a new business development. There was just the single line of about half a dozen houses, poorly lit by a lone streetlight. The B & B itself was equally unwelcoming, with peeling paintwork and litter filling the front yard. The negative impression deepened when Robin noted the flimsy padlock which secured the door to Penn's room. A TV could be heard blasting from further along the landing. Given that Penn had already paid for the room, the owner's bad temper at their departure seemed uncalled for. As the car sped them through the dark terraced streets towards home, Robin kept up a monologue on the probable joys and sorrows of life at the B & B, pleased at last to bring a watery chuckle from Penn. "That's my girl," she said encouragingly, "we'll soon have you right."

It didn't take long to get Penn settled in to the larger of the two attic bedrooms; after all, she had little in the way of belongings to put away. Robin gave her a quick rundown on the idiosyncrasies of the bathroom and kitchen appliances, all of which were leftovers from her aunt's days. Then she took her firmly back upstairs and said, "Bed, young woman. I want you fit to play tomorrow!"

"Thanks, Coach. I really appreciate this." Penn's voice was soft and she looked suddenly vulnerable, more like fifteen than twenty-three. "The name's Robin," Robin said as she bent and gave her a quick peck on the cheek. "Sleep tight."

Lying in the dark, listening to the unfamiliar sounds of the house, Penn wondered what had prompted her to spill out all the details in such an unaccustomed manner. She came to the conclusion it must have something to do with the way Robin's concern felt so warm and comforting. She swallowed hard as she remembered her mother's reaction. "How dare you?" she'd hissed, "and after all Stan's done for you."

"But, Mum," Penn tried again, only to be cut short.

"Don't you 'but' me, young lady. Ungrateful is what you are, downright selfish, I'd say. He gives you a roof over your head, food on the table, even lets you continue this nonsense of a career in football," she snorted scornfully, "as if that'll ever bring any money in to pay for your keep. And what do you do? Set upon him like a maniac!"

Penn remained dumbstruck with the injustice of her mother's accusations, yet unable to find a way to convince her of the other side of her husband's character. She longed for the closeness they'd had before Stan had come between them. Her silence was interpreted as insolence. Her mother's expression grew darker still. "Well, you'll just have to learn the hard way, then. You're certainly old enough. If this house isn't to your liking, then you better find one that is! You can leave right now, and I don't want you back 'til you can keep a civil tongue in your head." With this her mother folded her arms firmly across her chest and stood waiting by the front door. It was a matter of a few minutes for Penn to pack a bag. Not a word more was said.

5

The days had passed quickly since Penn had moved in, Robin realised with surprise. And it was much longer than that since anyone else had stayed at the house. Not since Mary, she reflected, wondering fleetingly why it was she had not felt the need to take another lover in the intervening months. Penn had revealed a talent for cooking, offering her services in lieu of the payment which Robin still refused. She'd accepted the delicious food, and was beginning to worry about its effect on her trim figure. It was for that reason she had begun to work out more earnestly than usual.

She also just seemed to be more full of get up and go these days. "Must be the approach of spring," she panted, as she jogged up the final steep incline to the front door. As she opened the door, she could smell the bacon. How had she ever managed before Penn arrived? It wasn't only the cooking. There were many other effects Penn produced around the house. Flowers appeared on the tables, brought in from the garden, the kitchen was clean and the dishes done regularly. Every time the weather allowed, Penn hung the washing out in the garden to dry.

"Don't make me too comfortable," Robin joked, "I might never let you leave."

Penn just grinned at her and continued to do as she pleased. It was easy to see she genuinely enjoyed the housekeeping tasks, so Robin let her go on, ignoring the slight warning bells at the back of her mind.

"Big day today." She looked at Penn across the table, the remains of the breakfast scattered between them. The morning sun was streaming in through the large window behind Penn, creating a halo effect around her cropped head. Robin thought, not for the first time, that Penn was quite a striking young woman in her own way. "Are you ready for it, Penn?"

Opposite her the blond head bobbed in the affirmative, eyes alight. "I just hope I don't let you down, Coach. You're putting a lot of faith in me." Penn still persisted in using the formal title, and Robin had given up trying to dissuade her after a couple of days.

"I know," she agreed with Penn, "but it's going to be fully justified. Don't forget I've been there. I know the standard you have to reach for the top clubs. You've got what it takes, Penn. And remember, we'll all be there rooting for you."

As expected, Penn blushed at the compliment and dropped her gaze to the dishes. "I'll clear these away," she said. "You go on and take a shower, I'll get one after you're done."

"Yes, ma'am." Robin teased as she went out of the kitchen and bounded up the stairs. Moments later she was under the shower, humming as she recalled her own trial session all those years ago. She'd been younger than Penn, just seventeen, eager and frisky as a colt. And Robin had to admit to herself, she'd been absolutely brimming with confidence. She was good and she knew it, although she always worked hard too, and took advice from senior players. "*Not a bighead, just a bit cocky.*" She grinned as the memories unwound.

She had played like a woman possessed during the seven-a-side tournament, focused on nothing but the dream of a training place with her beloved Deepdale Town. They'd been top of the league then, not like now, although at least she'd pulled them back up into the top half this season. She scored in every round, and came out on the winning team. Sally, watching from the sidelines, cheered herself hoarse. The scouts from all the other clubs chased after her, but she had eyes only for Bess Ingram from the Town. Her heart almost stopped when she saw Bess walking away in the opposite direction. She couldn't have failed, could she? It was one of the few moments of real doubt in her entire career and she held on to Sally to stop herself fainting with fear. Then Bess came over, bringing the photographer of the local paper with her, and the world had returned to its usual orbit.

It had taken her a year to get into the first team, partly because her parents insisted that she also finish her A-levels. She hadn't thanked them for that at the time, but they'd been right. More far-sighted than their hot-headed daughter, they foresaw the possibility of injury and made sure she was at least minimally equipped to do something else if the worst happened. Their insistence was the cause of some spectacular arguments. Robin paused in her brisk towelling down of her body.

The thought of her parents, as always, gave rise to mixed emotions. The love she felt for them was overlaid by a deep hurt and resentment. The arguments over her A-levels were mild compared to those that followed the disclosure of her sexuality. They just would not accept that she was a lesbian, continually dropping hints about grandchildren and discussing eligible men. Perversely, they always spoke very highly of Sally, turning a blind eye to her partner. Robin argued, begged, explained and finally yelled at them in angry desperation at their refusal to see her as herself. Wounding words were said as the fabric of family unity had ripped and torn under the strain. She'd hardly seen or spoken to her parents since, at least not voluntarily, not even when Sally offered to go with her.

"You have to face them sometime, love," Sally had said in her quiet way. And Robin agreed, "But just not yet, please, I need more time." Maybe this year they would succeed in bridging the gulf between them.

Realising she hadn't yet finished drying, Robin lifted one leg onto the side of the bath, and bent forward, towel in her hands, when she was surprised by Penn, half-naked, coming through the door. "Oh! I'm sorry! I thought you'd finished." Penn blushed scarlet, standing stock still a moment before retreating. "It was so quiet and the door was open, I'm sorry." She turned and fled, leaving Robin no time to react.

Penn's inadvertent invasion did not trouble her. She had no shame about her nakedness. She knew her body was in excellent condition, slim, strong and supple. No, it wasn't that which left her motionless, towel hanging loosely from her hands. It was what she saw in Penn's eyes, and the sudden flash of answering desire she felt in her belly. She hoped to god Penn hadn't seen that in her own eyes. For Penn was unable to remove her gaze from Robin's naked body quite quickly enough. For a couple of seconds her wide-open blue eyes took stock of Robin, moving quickly over her breasts and stopping at the dark triangle of her pubic hair. Robin recognised the expertise in the look instantly. It was after all her own first instinct in similar circumstances, although Penn was young to have gathered such experience. "*So that's the way the wind blows,*" she thought, "*that's going to complicate matters considerably unless I can stop it.*"

She moved briskly, towelling off the rest of her body. Putting on her robe, she knotted it firmly at her waist. She trod up the attic stairs and knocked softly at Penn's door. "Can I come in?"

Taking the answering groan as an affirmative she pushed the door open and took in the scene. Penn was lying on the bed, face pushed into the pillow. Robin sat beside her and rested a hand on her shoulder.

"Hey, it's not the end of the world," she said lightly. "I've been caught naked in a shower in worse circumstances, you know." Penn's voice was muffled, "I thought you'd finished, Coach, honest I did." Even in this extremity, Robin noticed wryly, the "Coach" epithet was not dislodged.

"Come on. Up you get." She took control, realising with relief that her own desire remained unnoticed. The situation was redeemable, if only she could keep it that way. She raised Penn off the pillow, pulling her round into the circle of her arms.

"Penn, Penn, you idiot. It's nothing to get upset about. I just forgot to shut the door. It comes of living alone." Penn drew a deep breath, the red receding from her cheeks, and began to regain control. She sat up a little, moving away from Robin, who let her go.

"I'm used to the changing room showers." Robin reminded her. "A little nudity doesn't shock me, not even quite a lot of it, actually." This time the light-hearted touch worked as Penn tutted at her and broke into a wavering grin herself.

"Sorry, Coach," she said again. "I must be more nervous than I thought. I'm usually pretty unshockable too. But I shouldn't have invaded like that. You've given up a lot of space, letting me stay here, I didn't mean to invade your privacy as well."

"You take up hardly any space at all." Robin reassured her quickly, and they were back to normal again, the crisis safely over. She glanced at the clock beside the bed. "Better get a move on, love. We need to leave in twenty minutes." And she went out of the door as Penn picked up her own towel, following behind her as far as the bathroom, taking extra care to close the door.

Robin dressed slowly. *"I need to watch myself,"* she admitted. She was determined Penn should not feel, once again, that she had to leave home. The word home rang a mental alarm bell. *"It's Penn being here which makes it feel so much a home."*

For a minute or two Robin's imagination ran free; she saw the two of them breakfasting under the blossom trees in the garden, chatting easily of plans to move plants or reshape the lawn. But bringing home her casual lovers for the odd night was one thing, setting up house with one quite another. *"Not that Penn's my lover, nor likely to be. I never mix work and pleasure,"* she reminded herself coolly. *"There's no way I can cope with the complication. I'll just forget I saw anything."* Penn was much too valuable an asset to the team to waste by taking any risks, or doing anything that might scare her away.

Robin's guiding principle was based in bitter experience. In her playing days, when she and Jude were both in the Town's first team squad, Hilary Wadham, their coach had had no such scruples. Jude was briefly infatuated with the coach who took full advantage of her position, unscrupulously exploiting Jude's vulnerability to the full. When the attraction faded, or as Robin believed more cynically, Hilary was no longer amused by Jude's devotion, it was Jude who suffered the jibes and teasing of the other team members. It took some time for Robin to pull her through.

By the time Penn came down, Robin had dismissed her daydreaming as irrelevant. They left for the trials in good order, meeting up with the other cars as planned. Robin's thoughts turned to the work ahead and she began to plan her final advice for Penn.

6

Penn watched Robin talking with Jude, the coach from Burnden United. In contrast to Robin's height, Jude Maine was a stocky, muscular woman, a shape that matched the reputation she'd earned in her playing days as a midfield dynamo. Jude had a rounded face, well weathered by years of outdoor activity, her usual expression of good humour given a hint of severity by the iron grey of her short wavy hair. Penn continued her warm-up routine. Her mind kept drifting and the image of Robin in the shower resurfaced, bringing with it a quickening of her pulse and breathing. She'd nearly made a complete ass of herself this morning, she reflected, but Robin's effect on her was powerful. For the umpteenth time she wondered what Robin made of her intrusion. Whatever she felt she was hiding it well, but Penn thought she detected a slight gleam of interest.

Despite her appearance of youth and vulnerability, Penn was something of a free spirit and a persistent optimist. She'd weathered her share of difficulties, not least of which was the battle with her stepfather. Her body tensed briefly at the memory. Since leaving home, she'd thought hard about her mother's lack of belief, eventually assuming that, as she was never the object of it, her mother truly could not accept that Stan had this side to his nature. She called her mother occasionally, when she knew he'd be at work and by keeping off touchy subjects they managed to talk well enough. Penn had not given up on persuading her mother of the truth, she was just biding her time. However much she wanted acknowledgement of the truth of her accusations, she knew she couldn't force her mother to see her point of view. And she could not bear to think of her mother reaching this conclusion through personal experience. For now, she resolved to leave her mother to her own opinions.

All things considered, life was pretty good. Penn felt confident of her chances in the trial and knew a professional career would open up for her if she did well. She loved the game, playing incessantly with a football for as long as she could remember, either by herself or with whoever else was willing. The game was as fresh and exciting to her now as it had been during her school years. She revelled in an accurate pass, a well planned tactical move, a strong, clean tackle and most of all in a well-placed shot. She would gladly put in hours of dedicated practice. She knew talent alone was not enough; hard work, and luck, too, were needed if she wanted to make football her career.

That thought brought her back to Robin again, who she knew would be giving Jude an honest assessment of her potential. As a coach, she could not be beaten, Penn thought, always quick to praise and encourage but never holding back when criticism was justified. It was a rare combination. It appeared she had her whole life sorted, but Penn sensed tensions underneath Robin's assured surface. Robin intrigued her. She wanted to know what went on inside that beautiful head. Why did she find it so hard to trust, to open up to others? True, she had close friends like Sally and Jude, both of whom Penn had met in the bar. As Penn saw it, Robin felt secure on the field or in the bar, but she rarely strayed outside of these two environments. What was she afraid of?

If asked, she could not have said exactly what made her think this, she had no concrete evidence. It was just intuition, but Penn's intuition rarely let her down. She herself was fanatical in her commitment to football, but she knew that there was plenty to enjoy beyond the sidelines. Penn saw no reason to restrict her interests or activities; she was always ready for a new experience. Nor did she shrink from the challenge of being 'out' in society at large. She took people as she found them, and most responded in the same way. She neither hid nor flaunted her sexuality.

There was a loud blast on a whistle and the loudspeaker crackled to life, instructing players, coaches and spectators to take up their stations. Penn finished her warm-up and with a wave in response to Robin's encouraging gesture, moved to join the other hopefuls, her mind focused on the games ahead.

The trials were organised by the four regional professional clubs, and were run like a knock-out competition. The players formed up into seven-a-side teams as instructed: existing players from the professional teams filled any positions for which nobody was being trialed. Each game lasted an hour, thirty minutes each way, and to reach the final, successful teams played a total of three games. As the number of teams grew less, trial players were swapped from one team to another, replacing the professionals whose skills were not in question. Penn found it a little unsettling to start each game with different team-mates but at least she was kept in the same position in the central midfield. Some of the other women on trial were moved about, playing on the left in one game, then the right in the next. Playing seven-a-side on full-size pitches meant the game flowed much more quickly as the players exploited the extra space, and by the last game Penn could feel her legs protesting, but it was a satisfying ache.

7

The evening sun still brought a little warmth to the corner of the garden where Penn and Robin sat, the remains of a hastily put together meal on the table in front of them. Robin was utterly relaxed, the peace of the garden regenerating her spirits. Spring flowers filled the beds around their feet with nodding yellow and purple colour. Above them the buds were swelling on the trees, eager to burst into life. Penn stretched luxuriously, feeling the pull of well-used muscles. It had been a glorious day. She grinned, and Robin lifted an enquiring eyebrow. "You look like a cat with the cream," she said, grinning herself. "I wonder why that might be?"

"Well," answered Penn, "it may just have something to do with the fact that I played brilliantly today. I don't see how Jude can resist offering me a place at United, do you?"

Shaking her head Robin said, "I did tell her you were good, but even I didn't expect you to get a hat-trick in two of the games. But it's not in the bag just yet, some of the others ran you close. It will depend on what she's looking for to build the team." Seeing Penn's grin fade slightly, she softened. "I know she needs an attacking mid-fielder, Penn, that's why I was keen for you to enter the trials now. It's about ninety-nine percent certain you'll be offered a place."

"Then a celebratory drink is not out of place. How about going down to the bar? I need to unwind a bit more."

"Give me a minute to clear this lot up and I'll be right with you."

They left ten minutes later, Penn breathing deeply with a feeling of rising excitement. It wasn't exactly a date, but she'd asked Robin to come and here they were. She knew she'd have to play it carefully to catch Robin, but after the morning and then the success of the trials, she felt anything was possible.

The bar was middling busy. There were the usual bunch around the pool table, in the area which also doubled as stage or dance floor, and most of the small, round tables had occupants. Sally and Ingrid welcomed them eagerly, wanting to know immediately how the trials went. Penn endured the limelight for a time, accepting the admiration of the group which included Robin. After a while the conversation moved on to other matters; the bar, and a recent local scandal involving the 'outing' of a supposedly lesbian councillor. Some members of the group felt it only right that those in public life should be made visible.

"But you have to think of the effect on the rest of their life," Robin argued. "It's not fair to push people into a public position before they're ready. It can do a lot of damage."

"It's only going to change if those in public places come out, though, isn't it?" another woman challenged. "There's not really that much resistance now and the more visible we are the less prejudice and ignorance can flourish."

To Penn's surprise Robin's answer was far sharper than the chatty nature of the conversation warranted. "Well, I happen to think people should be allowed their privacy, there's more discrimination than some of you think. Coming out is a personal decision. It's not for anyone else to force the pace."

Robin tasted the bitterness of such betrayal sharp on her tongue, even after eight years. She and Lucy had shared everything. She had told Lucy her inmost secrets, her hopes, dreams, excitements and fears, and there were plenty of all of them. She'd opened her heart and her body to Lucy knowing both would be safely held in loving hands. But Lucy had other ideas, not to mention ambition. She had taken all that Robin gave, then wrote about it in graphic detail for a national newspaper. Her sensational exposé of lesbians in football made Lucy's name as a journalist. She never looked back to see the devastation wreaked upon Robin by the three-day wonder the article had stirred up. Robin shuddered as she recalled the desperation of those months. Lucy's face rose clearly in her mind's eye, dark hair framing her elfin features. How Robin had loved to stare into those eyes, so dark a brown as to be almost black, and, she had thought, so breathtakingly honest.

Journalism was as important to Lucy's life as football was to Robin's. She was forever on the alert for a story. Even sitting on the bus, a chance remark would set Lucy off on an idea. The journey would whizz by as her hilarious chatter entertained Robin. It had all seemed harmless enough. Most of Lucy's articles were the sort of hard luck stories which made up the bread and butter business of any small local paper. She had a flair for making the connection between these minor upsets and the wheeling and dealing of local politics, often to the detriment of the politicians; but Robin had never seen malice in any of her articles. She still couldn't believe how mistaken she had been.

With an effort she brought her thoughts back to the conversation. "It is important tho', isn't it? I mean here we are in every walk of life, blending in without notice, and yet it's because we don't stand out that people can say whatever they like about us and get away with it. We have to do something." This remark came from a vivacious woman with an impressive array of nose and ear rings.

"That's true," one of the younger women agreed. "I get a real thrill from seeing someone standing there in public, just saying, yes, I'm a lesbian - so?"

An older woman spoke, more cautiously, "I don't think there is an easy answer, is there? We could talk about it forever and still it would make no difference. It's hard to have to make an issue of our sexuality all the time. There's more to life, isn't there?"

Penn, noticing how withdrawn Robin had become, attempted to lighten the discussion. "Well, I don't know about that. I think sex is pretty important! And judging by the number of people with an interest in 'top-shelf' videos down at the store, that goes for lots of people!"

This brought a burst of laughter along with a ribald request. "Go on then, tell us the best blue movies around. Do you get viewing privileges with your job, too?"

"What's your speciality interest?" Penn countered. "There's straightforward threesomes, they're always popular, then there's fantasy, anything from leather and chains to desert islands. And there's probably more I haven't seen. I mean, that I haven't seen anyone take out!" she added quickly, gratified to see Robin's face lighten as hilarity engulfed the women round the table. As the group began to dissolve, her eye was caught by the empty pool table.

"Quick, Coach, let's get on it while there's a gap. I'll bet you a pound I can lick you in a best-of-five." It was a challenge she knew Robin would find irresistible, and her bait was taken without hesitation.

The rest of the bar receded from Penn's consciousness as she focused on the plain and spotted balls of the pool table. Robin was good, a solid accurate player, but Penn had audacity, going for risky shots. She missed some, naturally, but hit her target often enough to make it a viable strategy. At two games apiece, the tension mounted. A crowd gathered around the table, each combatant with her own group of supporters commenting gleefully on skill and exclaiming in agony at each miss. Halfway through, Robin's eyes met hers across the table and Penn was delighted to see her a little discomfitted. *"Yes,"* she said inwardly, *"there's more to me than meets the eye, Robin Goodison."*

There was a cheer as Robin potted her last ball. "Only the black and I've got you," she crowed, bowing flamboyantly over her cue.

"Don't go counting any chickens, Coach," Penn muttered, lining up another risky shot. With two balls still to go, it was now or never. She bit her lip in concentration, squinted down the cue, shut out the doubters in the crowd and hit the ball sweetly into the corner pocket. The bonus was a lucky ricochet off the black, leaving her perfectly positioned for the last ball. In it went and a collective breath was expelled around her.

She straightened up. "Got your pound ready, Coach?" she quizzed, then bending with a flourish she smoothly potted the black to loud applause.

Robin already had the pound on the table, but before Penn could pick it up she added another two. "Double or quits. One more game?"

Penn didn't hesitate, moving to set the balls up again. She was exultant. Robin was really competing now, showing more respect for her erstwhile protÈgÈe. And about time too, thought Penn.

There was an expectant hush as a coin was tossed to determine who played first. Robin won and the game began. The crowd was watching more intensely now, their comments softly voiced to avoid disturbing the players' concentration, each shot applauded or criticised according to results. This time it was Penn who potted her balls first and had a chance to sink the black while Robin still had a ball on the table. As usual, Penn went for the more risky shot but this time it didn't pay off. The way was open for Robin. Moving slowly and deliberately she lined up her last two pots with deadly accuracy. The applause was loud and long as Robin made the most of her victory, holding out an imperious hand for Penn's payment, which was made with a smile.

Seeing that the entertainment was over for the night, the crowd drifted away towards the bar. Still playing the magnanimous conqueror, Robin asked, "Can I get you a drink as runner-up, now that I'm so flush?" Penn nodded, grinning wickedly. "You certainly can, mine's a whisky with ice, thanks."

The next hour passed quickly. Penn could never remember what they talked about, just that she felt a subtle change in their relationship. Robin was taking her more as an equal, dropping the almost imperceptible air of seniority she'd kept up through the weeks of sharing the house. Penn's spirits rose. She was acutely aware of how Robin's body moved under her clothes, remembering her nakedness in the shower that morning. She crossed her fingers under the table and made a fervent wish.

8

Penn shut the door and followed Robin into the sitting room. "What about a coffee, Coach?" Seeing Robin begin to refuse, she added quickly, "one late night isn't going to do any damage. It *is* Sunday tomorrow."

"OK then. Just a small one." Robin flopped into her favourite armchair, idly watching Penn through the doorway. As Penn waited for the coffee machine to finish its noisy frothing, she considered ways to extend the evening just that little bit more. She carried the two brimming cappuccinos through the door and handed Robin hers, careful not to let their hands touch. She didn't want to jump the gun.

They chatted easily for a while. Penn, unable to find a natural way to bring them closer together, did not quite have the courage for a direct move. Robin rose and went through to the kitchen, taking the cups with her. "I'll just do these," she said "then I'm off to bed."

"I'll dry," said Penn. Then, as Penn reached for the tea-towel, Robin turned to pick up a cup from the table. They bumped together and reached automatically to keep from falling. Robin's arm went around Penn's waist, and Penn's hands held Robin's shoulders.

"Oops!" - then silence as their eyes met, inches apart.

As if in slow motion their mouths drew closer; lips touched, tentatively to begin with and then with deepening hunger. Penn's heart raced. Her hands caressed Robin's back, holding her closer as the kiss continued. She felt her nipples harden. Robin too was breathing raggedly. Still embracing they moved to the couch. Penn felt Robin's full weight upon her and lifted her hips in response. Clothes were discarded, skin slid over skin, warm and smooth to the touch. Penn caught Robin's hair and pulled her mouth down against her own, drinking in her taste. "Touch me," she commanded urgently. Robin obeyed. Her touch was as Penn had imagined, sure and swift bringing her to a tumultuous climax. Temporarily sated, she languidly reached for Robin, eager to respond to the need she'd felt. There was no rush. They had all night now.

Her peace was shattered almost immediately as Robin, stiffening beside her, seemed suddenly to snap awake as if from a dream. She looked at the clothes on the floor, then at Penn. "Oh god. Oh no. Shit! I never meant ..." Her voice faded. Penn struggled to sit up, reaching for Robin, only to be pushed away. "No Penn, I can't. It's not right, can't you see? We can't do this."

Penn was stunned. "What do you mean ... ? Do what ... ? I thought you ... ." Penn, too, could not finish a coherent sentence.

"Penn. Listen to me. I'm your Coach, you're a player in the team. I can't get involved with you this way. It won't work. Please try to understand ... it's just wrong." Robin's desperation was obvious. She moved quickly, gathering and replacing her clothes, urging Penn to do the same.

Automatically Penn did as she was bid, her body functioning while her mind tried to assimilate the situation. Nothing felt wrong to her. It had never felt so wonderful. But, she realised, Robin wasn't referring to their lovemaking; her concern lay elsewhere. She needed to unravel what Robin had said. She deliberately caught Robin's hand, stopping her rapid movements.

"What exactly is wrong?" Her voice was calm. This was very important. She was certain the evening's rapport between them had been real, something which could be built on and nurtured; she wasn't about to lose that possibility through panic.

Robin looked at her, fearing the usual emotional outburst of a youngster, but was reassured by Penn's outward calm. She took a deep breath, searching her mind to find the least painful way of putting it. She ignored the tingle in her arm produced by Penn's touch.

"It's not you, Penn, please don't think that. I like you, you're a lovely girl, but I can't be your lover." The word sounded strange to her own ears. "It's unprofessional. I don't know why I let this happen. I must have been mad." Seeing Penn flinch, she rushed on, "I'm sorry I didn't mean it to sound like that. We have to be members of a team, Penn, I can't single you out, treat you differently, worry about you more than the others. It wouldn't be fair, and they'd be sure to work out what was going on. It's impossible to hide. You do see that, don't you?"

Penn nodded, not trusting herself to speak. Robin held both her hands, facing her, looking straight into her eyes. "It can't happen again, Penn. We have to forget all about it. Put it right out of our minds." Robin's voice was still urgent, but her grip relaxed when Penn nodded again.

"Yes, I see," Penn finally managed to say, feeling bewildered, her senses still full of the power of Robin's body and her own response to it. But it was true, she did see the point Robin was making, the awkwardness she was afraid of.

"OK. Good girl. That's alright then. No harm done. Goodnight." And with that Robin fled upstairs to bed.

Penn followed slowly. She had a lot to think about. It was another few weeks to the end of the season. If she got the place at Burnden United, then Robin would no longer be her coach, her professional concern no longer relevant. *"It's up to me,"* Penn thought. *"It's only postponed, not called off. I just need to behave myself for the next few weeks, pretend nothing's happened, show Robin she can trust me. Then we can start again."* With this cheering thought Penn followed Robin upstairs.

9

Robin lay awake for some time, tossing and turning, unable to put her mind at rest. *"I should have seen it coming. The signs were clear enough this morning, for god's sake. I'm a bloody fool."* She was both appalled and exhilarated as she recalled the scene downstairs. Penn's body delighted her, its strength and suppleness, her immediate response to Robin's intuitive caresses. The force of her own desire caught her completely off guard. She shook her head as if to dislodge the memories. This could not be. She had made her golden rule long ago and, until tonight, never broken it. "Coaching and sex don't mix." She repeated the phrase like a protective mantra, over and over.

Jude's career was nearly destroyed by the selfishness of Hilary Wadham, the former coach at Deepdale Town. Robin could still feel the stony atmosphere in the changing room after Hilary spent most of one half-time talk concentrating only on Jude's contribution, ignoring both the other goal-scorer and the keeper who'd made an outstanding save. There were many dark looks and barbed comments. Even after the short affair was over, the rest of the team always maintained a slight reserve in Jude's company. Robin's efforts kept the worst from her, but only moving to a new club fully restored Jude's confidence.

She was honest enough to admit that Penn succeeded in getting under her skin in a way no-one had for a long time. She'd enjoyed the evening and the way their friendship was deepening. Penn had qualities that were not apparent on the football pitch. She had a freshness Robin found endearing. There was her youth, of course, but this was something deeper, more lasting. Penn approached the world with an openness Robin envied, at ease with herself and sure of her acceptance wherever she found herself. Robin found her captivating company, was drawn in and wanted more.

That sense of growing friendship, of slow exploration and discovery, was one which Robin did not want to lose. It was not going to be easy to re-establish. Penn seemed to accept her withdrawal, reacting far less strongly than Robin anticipated. In fact she took it very calmly, Robin thought. Maybe, for Penn, lovemaking was less serious, an opportunity taken quickly when found, but as quickly let go. After all, Robin knew plenty of women like that.

Taking a rather bitter comfort from this thought, she tried to disregard the intensity of her own response, the way Penn's body danced under her touch. It was just a brief encounter. There was no deeper meaning. There would be no need to mention it again, no need to fret over any damage done. Life would return to normal in the morning. No need to make a mountain out of a molehill.

But such thoughts did little to help her relax. Recognising the source of her tension she turned over and let her hand slip down between her thighs. In a while she fell into a fitful sleep.

_10_

The end of the football year always came as a shock to Robin, springing upon her from what seemed the distant future. This year was no exception, just more triumphant than usual. The Town's women's team added a second piece of silverware to the shelf over the changing room door by winning their division of the League. Today was the last match. They needed victory against Westhampton City, away from home, and achieved it with surprising ease. As usual, Penn was instrumental in the victory, providing both strength in defence and inspiration for attack. They'd have a hard time finding a replacement now it was certain she was moving to join Burnden United. Her game had improved still further since the trials where she performed with such brilliance. Robin had every confidence that she'd hear plenty about this member of her team in the future, possibly even on the international stage. She felt pride in playing her small part in establishing what should be a long and successful career.

The buzz behind her in the darkened bus died down as the young women drifted into sleep. This was the longest journey they made in a season, well over two hundred miles each way. It would be late when they got back, probably close to midnight. Robin sat thinking ahead to the end-of-season celebrations planned for the following evening. She'd better do some work on her speech. The formality of such occasions was daunting. It was the only aspect of being the team's coach which she disliked. She needed to psych herself up beforehand, usually enlisting Sally's help in getting the right touch to the speech. Her own choice of words was better suited to the changing room than the ballroom. She had most of the speech worked out. It was just the inclusion of a reference to Penn's imminent departure that was eluding her. Maybe if she just let her mind float for a while, inspiration would come. She let the hum of the engine lull her, and fell asleep.

The sudden quiet woke her some hours later as Jenny, their regular driver, cut the engine. "We're home, girls," she announced to the sleeping passengers behind her. Robin leant forward.

"Sorry Jenny, I didn't mean to leave you to do it all yourself. You should have woken me."

"You needed the rest more than me, love," Jenny said, her voice cheerful. "Anyway I can catch up in the morning. Bill's taken the kids to his mum's for the weekend. We planned ahead for once." She grinned, the chaos of her home life well known to Robin, who hugged her briefly round the shoulder.

"Thanks anyway," Robin said. She stretched, then moved back through the bus, shaking the young dreamers awake.

She waited, making sure each one was collected or seen safely onto a bus, before picking up the kit bag and taking Penn's arm. "You too," she said. "Time to get you home to bed." Penn yawned hugely, leaning lightly against her while she fished for the key.

"It's in your other pocket, I think," she mumbled sleepily, surprising Robin once again. Sure enough, the key was there. Robin opened the car door and guided Penn through, protecting her head as she stumbled slightly.

"God, I'm tired," she said and faded off to sleep again almost before Robin was behind the wheel.

Robin, also more tired than she realised, forced her mind to concentrate on the road. But she was highly conscious of Penn's body beside her. Her guard slipping, her thoughts shifted in a direction she quickly censored when more alert. It was weeks since the fateful day of the trials, but Robin had found it a struggle to act out the uncomplicated role of coach to player friendship she'd assigned herself. Now she wished she could find some way out. Her feelings for Penn were far from simple friendship, neither were they those of the team coach for her star player. She couldn't describe them as complicated, however. What she felt was straightforward and intense sexual desire. That desire grew in strength rather than diminished for lack of nourishment. And there was no encouragement from Penn. She had taken Robin at her word, never pressing for a repetition of their brief sexual encounter, returning to the warm but definitely platonic friendship without apparent difficulty.

Robin was not finding it so easy to keep her feelings under control. She took extra care in the house, keeping clear space between them, avoiding chance encounters by careful design. She was not about to admit to unrequited passion, although the energy it took to conceal her feelings was exhausting. The obvious option of arranging for Penn to stay elsewhere was never even considered.

Only Sally knew the full strength of her feelings. Late one evening after the bar closed, she surprised Robin staring morosely into a glass of whisky. Knowing Robin was not a natural spirits drinker she sensed that something was amiss. "Heart trouble?" she questioned quietly. "Another one of your admirers playing up?"

Robin groaned, "Not exactly."

Sally noted that there hadn't been any romantic exploits of late; was her friend a reformed character, then? Was that the cause of her misery? Sally had always been able to cajole Robin into loosening up and letting go of what troubled her.

But, as Robin unfolded her problem, Sally's expression became more serious. "You've got it bad, haven't you love?" she said.

Robin nodded, near to tears. "I've never had it this way, Sal. Not like this. I ache every night with wanting her." She bent her head onto her friend's shoulder. "What am I going to do?" she moaned.

"Just hold on in there, Robin love, something'll come up. When the feeling's this strong it always comes through in the end. Don't give up." She hugged her fiercely. It had been a long time coming, Sally thought, but she'd always known Robin would fall hard when it did. She hoped desperately that her words would come true, but while there was every chance that Penn would enjoy a love affair, it was much harder to know whether she would want anything more than that.

"Penn, wake up." Robin shook her passenger gently, then a little harder as Penn only turned and settled more firmly into the curve of the seat. "Come on, love, we're home."

Penn's eyes opened with the unfocused gaze of a very young child, causing Robin's heart to flip over in her chest. Robin had already taken in the kit, leaving the sleeping Penn till the last moment. She wanted only to study the lovely young face, softened with sleep, feeling a strong desire to kiss the sensual lips. She took Penn's hand and pulled her to her feet, then, with an arm around her slight waist, guided her through the front door and up the stairs to her room. Sitting her down on the side of the bed Robin bent and removed her shoes and socks. She pulled her jersey over her head, acutely aware of Penn's breasts as she leaned sleepily against her. Laying her gently on her bed and folding back the duvet, Robin was about to slip her legs around and under the covers when she became aware of a change.

She turned her head, looking directly at Penn and found herself staring straight into those deep-set blue eyes. She sat completely still, frozen, knowing her thoughts could be read easily, wanting to turn and run and wanting to stay. Penn sat up slowly, her eyes never leaving Robin's, until only inches separated them. A slight smile played over her lips with just a hint of the triumphant in it. "Caught you!" she whispered and put her mouth over Robin's.

Penn's hands were under her shirt, her fingers circling Robin's erect nipples. In a moment Penn removed both their shirts, Robin felt Penn's skin soft and warm against her own, teeth nipping at the lobes of her ear as Penn nuzzled into her neck. Robin shuddered, pent up desire exploding all through her limbs. Her arms reached around Penn's waist, her fingers slipped under the tracksuit, pushing the material out of the way. Penn's hands were now in Robin's hair, pulling her head backwards so that she could plant a line of kisses along her collar-bone. Robin drew a sharp breath as Penn's hot mouth closed around her pulsing nipple.

"Penn," she said urgently, "I can't ... you mustn't ... I'm the coach, you're in the team ... we can't!" She tried to pull away, but was held firm.

"Not any more, I'm not," replied Penn, breathing hotly into her ear. "Today was the last game. Next season I'm playing for United ... remember?"

"By god, you're right. I'd forgotten, but still ... ." Robin's voice trailed away. She was unable to voice the deeper fear that her own emotion could swallow her whole, that she was losing control of her ordered existence. She wanted more than a casual affair with Penn, but that thought frightened her too.

Penn's lips left a trail of small kisses from one nipple to the other. Robin shut her eyes briefly, closed her mind to her anxieties, ceased thinking altogether, and opened them to find the world revolving on a new axis. Then she looked directly at Penn.

Penn glowed as she watched Robin's eyes travel over her body, followed by her hands, as Robin now responded willingly to her clear invitation. Robin cupped her hands around Penn's breasts. She had played out this scene so often in her dreams that each caress already seemed embedded in her memory. Her body quaked with the power unleashed between them, blotting out conscious thought.

A while later they lay, still tangled together, as the molten heat of their limbs cooled into separate solidities. Robin idly twisted her fingers into Penn's short hair. Penn shifted slightly, placing her head against Robin's shoulder with a sigh.

"You OK?" The question was soft.

Penn murmured "Mmmm." She didn't want to disturb their intimacy but Robin wriggled upwards, half-sitting. "I'd better leave you to sleep, I s'pose." Her hand strayed over Penn's head, betraying her reluctance to move away.

"Stay here with me, don't go, please." Penn pulled her back. Robin was easily persuaded, suddenly overtaken by a huge yawn as she lay back down, sinking into the combined warmth created by Penn and the duvet. She was asleep in no time, as was Penn beside her.

11

Robin woke slowly, stretching luxuriously. She was conscious of Penn's legs lying against her own, and as she breathed, the scent of her entered her nostrils. She opened her eyes to find Penn leaning above her, head propped on her bent arm, watching.

"Morning, Coach." This was said with a teasing smile, acknowledging that the term no longer strictly applied. "How about some breakfast?"

Robin reached out, tracing Penn's jaw-line with a fingertip. "Mmmm, I do feel the hunger pangs coming on. What are you offering?" Her fingers continued their lazy exploration, now circling Penn's nipple which hardened at her touch. "I'm sure you could tempt me with something." She looked up at Penn, her eyes darkening. She pulled Penn's willing body towards her.

The sun had moved further round the bedroom wall when Penn roused herself again. "I s'pose we better take a shower. D'you want to go first?" Deliberately teasing she continued, "I promise not to look," and dodged quickly to avoid the pillow aimed at her head.

Eventually, showered and dressed, they arrived in the kitchen. It was a fine early summer day with the sunlight slanting through the windows, which Penn opened wide.

"Let's eat in the garden."

The air was warm, buzzing with insects as the sun beat down into the sheltered corner where Penn sat. The blossom was now in its full glory, scenting the air all around. She watched Robin pottering a few yards away, pulling up the larger weeds, tidying some of the more sprawling plants. Penn loved the concentration on her face, the mouth slightly puckered, a small wrinkle between the dark eyebrows. It was the same expression Robin often wore during training sessions. Penn breathed deeply. She could not quite believe the events of the past twenty four hours. She was tempted to pinch herself just to prove this was no dream. She even felt she was beginning to break through Robin's inner reserve. Earlier on she'd asked Robin how she came by such a large house. From Robin's account, the aunt who'd left it to her sounded like a wonderfully forthright woman. Penn glanced at her watch. It was getting late.

"I don't like to remind you, Coach, but didn't you say something about finishing a speech for the annual dinner tonight?"

Robin glanced up, pushing her fringe back from her forehead and leaving an earthy mark in its place. She grimaced. "Damn," she swore softly, "I'd managed to forget that entirely, I can't stand all the formality. But I guess you're right, it has to be done." She came towards Penn absently wiping her hands on the seat of her trousers. "Care to give me a few ideas?"

"I can try," said Penn. "What have you got so far?"

"I had some notes somewhere, on the table in the spare room I think. I was working on it the other day." She followed Penn inside, and finding pen and paper, they set to work.

12

Robin pulled at her collar, shrugging her shoulders. She always felt such an idiot dressed up in formal wear. That was another reason she hated the club's annual end of season bash. Then there were the members of the director's board with their clumsy attempts at flirtation, not to mention the foxtrot. Still, the speech had been a good one. People laughed in the right places, many of those the result of Penn's assistance that afternoon.

Most of the team were present, gathered in two or three knots in corners of the room, many looking as uncomfortable in the setting as Robin herself felt. On any other day, she would join one of the groups but in this setting she felt she had to at least try and socialise. She found small talk difficult and many of the non-playing members knew little about the game, so football was a short-lived conversation topic.

Surreptitiously, she looked at her watch. Shit! It wasn't even nine o'clock yet. That meant at least another hour before it was respectable to depart. This formal entertainment suite, with its plush velvet, heavily styled furniture and large ornate mirrors, was the only part of the club's premises in which she did not feel at home. If it wasn't for the fact that, as the women's team coach, she had to attend the annual knees-up, she would never set foot in it. She drifted towards the bar, thankful to find one or two of the more knowledgeable members propping it up. She could talk tactics and prospects for next season with them.

"You've gathered a talented bunch together this year, Robin. It's good to see them bring in some rewards." The speaker was a woman often seen hosting business parties during the more prestigious matches.

"Yes, it's good to see quality players coming back to the Town," remarked a man Robin did not know by name. She agreed it was.

"But then again, it's not just players you need. There's a lot of others involved in creating a winning team, developing an environment in which individual skills can be given full rein. There's a lot to be said for a consistent pitch, that's never mentioned in all the celebrations, is it?" Bill Withers, long-standing season ticket holder and one time junior groundsman with the Town, loved holding forth with a captive audience. "Mind you, I suppose the coach might have something to do with it too," he said with a broad wink in Robin's direction. "And this year you got the success you deserve, eh Robin?"

"Thanks, Bill. It's not everyone who appreciates all the hard work I put in." Robin smiled. Bill was a well-loved character, an established part of the Town scenery.

"I s'pose this new-fangled video watching is meant to help you with the tactics, is it?" Bill sniffed loudly. "I never saw anything wrong with scouts myself. Don't understand how a machine can be better than a bloke with proper eyes in his head."

"It all comes down to money in the end, Bill." Henry Winterbottom, honorary treasurer of the supporters' club, joined the conversation. "You see, employing enough scouts to watch all the opposition teams costs a lot more than the TV network. And what's more, the cost of the network is spread around the whole league, and everyone benefits. It's a much better system, isn't it?" He turned to Robin for confirmation.

"I think Henry's right, Bill, 'tho' I can see your point about scouts. I still think they have their uses, but the video system is very versatile. You can go over games as many times as you want instead of relying on just the scout's memory. Provided the camera's well placed, it gives a comprehensive view of the game, too. With it being in every ground now, it's certainly handy to check back on a team's performance over a number of games in just an hour or two." Seeing that Bill remained unconvinced, Robin continued. "For us in the women's team it's invaluable; we've never had the funds for the scouts we'd need to watch all the other teams. But of course, you know why they really got it? So that we can watch all the matches we want without having to pay a penny!"

"Well now! I knew there had to be a catch to it somewhere," said Bill amid the general laughter. "Better not let those satellite people hear you saying that!"

During the lull in the conversation that followed, Robin spotted Penn on the other side of the room in animated conversation with the club treasurer and his wife. She had been ready to shelter Penn under a protective wing, introduce her to the friendlier faces, but no such necessity arose. Penn was adept at getting others to talk and seemed to know just which questions would set them off. It was a skill Robin herself was yet to develop she thought ruefully, though to be fair, Penn's interest was probably genuine. She did the same this morning, Robin mused, getting me to talk about the house and Aunt Edie. It wasn't a side of Penn that came out much on the field or in the changing room, although she held her end up in the general banter. Robin felt a flush of pleasure as she watched Penn move easily through the throng; the more she got to know this young woman, the more she liked and respected her.

13

The short weeks of the off-season flew by. Penn and Robin settled into a new routine as easily as they had when Penn first moved in. Penn worked at the video store, often putting in extra hours to build up her savings in anticipation of the move to United. While Robin had no actual training duties, she too was busy: renewing contracts, re-ordering and repairing equipment, improving training schedules, and, of course, supervising the bar.

"D'you fancy the pictures tonight?" Penn asked. "There's a new one I'd quite like to see but it's your turn really."

Penn loved action films with plenty of stunts and special effects. Robin's liking was for more thoughtful productions. She wanted to be intrigued by the story, to leave the cinema with her head still populated by the characters and the dilemmas they faced. With an initial toss of a coin, they had devised a system of alternating trips to the nearest multiplex for Penn and the smaller, art-house cinema for Robin.

"Is it explosions, crashes or natural disasters this time?" Robin enquired with a raised eyebrow. "And what do I get for allowing you an extra turn? I might need convincing."

"Well," Penn was thoughtful for a moment. "How can I tempt you ..."

"Very easily, as you should know by now." Robin came up beside her, wrapping her arms round Penn's waist and nuzzled the back of her neck. "You smell delicious. Couldn't we just stay in and amuse ourselves?"

Penn turned within the circle of Robin's arms. "Of course." She kissed Robin. "But I didn't realise this one was still on, I thought we'd missed it. I suppose it'll come round again, and there is always the video." She sighed, letting her face fall slightly.

Robin laughed. "Oh alright, we'll go! Who could deprive you of anything when you look like that? You're shameless!"

Penn brightened immediately, "I thought that's what you liked about me," she murmured suggestively.

At weekends, and sometimes to take advantage of the long summer evenings, they went out in the car. Robin loved to venture along the minor roads which wound back and forth through the dales, buried deep between constricting stone walls then bursting out into the vastness of the open moor. Sharing their mysteries with Penn made it more enjoyable still. At first she would do all the driving, reluctant to trust anyone with her beloved car, but Penn soon persuaded her that map-reading was not her strength.

"It was left there, that one you just went straight past. I told you it was coming up soon!" Her voice rising, Penn slapped the map against the dashboard.

"You did not! You said a few hundred yards not round the next bloody corner! How the hell am I supposed to make a turn when you don't give me any notice?"

"I did! I told you, you just don't listen." Penn snorted in disgust.

"Alright, alright, keep your hair on, dammit!" They drove in silence for a while, then Robin spoke more calmly. "Look, there's a nice little pub. Let's take a break." She pulled the car into the small car park and led the way inside. They settled in to a corner seat.

She could see Penn was still upset. "I'm sorry, love. I didn't mean to shout at you back there. It's difficult to tell exactly where you are sometimes, on these small roads. And the map is an old one."

Penn shrugged, not yet willing to be mollified. "I did tell you in time. You don't have to make excuses. I can read a map you know."

"Oh, Penn, I didn't mean that. Please, don't let it spoil the day. I don't want to argue with you." Robin took a long swallow of beer. "Tell you what, why don't you drive for a while and I'll struggle with the map?"

Penn looked at her in disbelief. "You mean you'd actually let me drive your car? Your pride and joy?"

Robin smiled. "You've got a license, haven't you? Well then, why not?"

"No, I don't think so. You'd only shout more, worrying about the damage I'll do." Penn shook her head. She knew exactly how much the car meant to Robin. The thought of the consequences, should she damage it, was unbearable.

"Do you make a habit of driving carelessly, then? You told me you'd never had an accident, not even while you had that delivery job. Come on, Penn, give it a try. I promise not to shout any more today. Please, just once, at least?"

"OK then, if you're sure." Penn recovered her good humour. She was a good driver, and anything was better than bickering about directions. "But one mistake on the map-reading, Coach, and you're for the high jump!"

So Robin became the navigator, reassured by Penn's smooth handling of the car. She gave her an early test on the trickiest of winding single track roads, during which Penn never crunched a gear or skidded an inch. Robin loved maps anyway and watching Penn's face as she concentrated on the traffic was no hardship.

"If we take the next one on the right, that should bring us out on the ridge in no time." Robin glanced out of the window at the setting sun. "Then we can walk about half a mile to the edge for the best view."

The sky was clear in the west where the sun dropped slowly towards the horizon, but with a sprinkling of cloud higher up which caught the changing colours: yellow, mauve, pink. Smoke from a field of burning stubble drifted across the scene, the silence punctuated only by the low moans of sheep or the rapid scolding of a retiring bird. They sat quietly for over an hour, absorbed in the spectacle. Penn lay back on the steep slope, supported by Robin's legs on either side, her head resting on Robin's stomach. Robin played with Penn's hair, an activity which was now habitual, her fingers stroking gently behind Penn's ears. It was a long time since she'd felt such deep contentment, but she kept that thought to herself.

14

Penn bounced into the living room, "You'll never guess what I found today." Her face beamed with pleasure. "I was browsing through the market, you know, the old junk stalls down at the end, near the canal. And I saw it, tucked away at the back. I just had to get it for you."

"Get what?"

"It's in the garden." Penn reached for Robin's hand and pulled her from the chair where she sat. "Come on. You have to see. It's absolutely perfect."

Robin followed her through to the breakfast room but before they went through the open doors to the garden Penn pulled her to a stop. "Just a minute. I don't want you to see it until you're in the right spot." She fetched a tea-towel from the kitchen and tied it around Robin's head covering her eyes. Then, taking her hand again, she led her down to the far corner of the garden. "OK. You can take it off now."

This part of the garden was overshadowed by a large beech tree in the neighbouring plot, but the shade was dappled rather than dark. Robin removed the tea-towel and looked around, letting her eyes readjust. Beside her, Penn hopped from foot to foot in anticipation. "Well? Do you like it?"

The "it" in question was a bird table in wrought iron standing about three feet high. The column was a replica of twisted ivy which then formed a wreath around the 'table'. This was in two parts. The lower stone table was slightly concave for water, and on the edge of the upper table sat two iron birds, heads cocked.

"Oh Penn. It's wonderful! You're right, it's absolutely perfect for this spot." Robin moved to examine it more closely. "But Penn, it must have cost a packet, and how did you get it in here all by yourself, it weighs a ton."

"It was a bit of a battle," Penn conceded, "but I wanted to have it in the right spot before you saw it. You do like it don't you?"

"I love it. You shouldn't have, really. But it's lovely, thank you, very much." Robin felt suddenly overwhelmed as she hugged Penn to her. "You don't have to buy me things, Penn." This was the latest in a series of unexpected gifts Penn had given her.

"I know that, but when I see things, I can't resist. And I love to watch you when you get a surprise." Penn laughed. "Anyway, it wasn't expensive, just a few quid, really, once I bargained with the guy on the stall. I persuaded him that reconstituted stone was the in thing now according to all the garden experts, and that I was his only chance to get rid of it."

"Well, you have impeccable taste, better than any so-called expert. Did you get any seed for it? I'll put some water in too." Robin hurried back into the house, quickly returning to fill the table with food and water. She spent much of the day creeping down the garden to see if the birds appreciated it as much as she did, dashing in to report to Penn each new variety of visitor.

15

Mrs Goodison put the apples into her carrier bag and straightened up to consult her list. Just the bread to get and she'd be done. The market was as busy as ever this Saturday morning despite the intermittent showers. The colourful striped canopies flapped and dripped in the damp breeze. She had never got into the habit of shopping at the supermarket on the edge of Deepdale, preferring the familiarity and intimacy of the market stalls. Besides, George would never accept that produce wrapped in plastic was as fresh as what came in a brown paper bag and she had long since given up arguing with him. Of course, she could park more easily out of town, and take the shopping right to the car in one of those confounded trolleys, but she rarely had that much to carry. The market was open on Wednesdays,

Fridays and Saturdays and with just the two of them she could manage easily by coming into town two or three times a week.

Although she rarely admitted it, even to herself, Mrs Goodison had another motive for frequenting the market so often. Her daughter's fondness for a particular variety of Wensleydale meant that Robin could often be seen in the queue alongside the cheese stall in the market. By visiting the market so often, Robin's mother could be sure to catch sight of her every few weeks, reassuring herself of Robin's health and wellbeing. Usually these glimpses had to suffice; she was unnerved by the abruptness of her daughter's responses if she approached to speak. Mrs Goodison could not progress beyond Robin's gruff 'yes' or 'no' answers into the conversation she longed for.

Once or twice she'd talked it all over with George and she knew he was right in his advice. "You've got to let her come round in her own good time, Jean" he said, pointing at her with the stem of his pipe. "Remember, she was just a youngster when it all blew up like that. She took it all very seriously, you know."

"I know, dear," she replied, "but she must know that we spoke without thinking, that it's her who's important to us, not who she ..." Mrs Goodison hesitated, a flush rising to her cheek. "I mean she knows how fond we are of Sally, doesn't she? That shows we're not prejudiced."

"Yes, she knows, but it's her pride that was hurt. Just give her time." And with that George would clamp his pipe back between his teeth and return his gaze to the newspaper, leaving her to struggle with the unresolved issues for herself. She took every legitimate opportunity to contact Robin, ringing her to ask about family matters which she made to sound important, or forwarding the few stray items of post which still came to the house and including a note of her own, but sometimes she despaired of ever breaking the deadlock. She knew Robin would be horrified to think her mother spied on her, or worse still used her friendship with Sally to gather news of her welfare. This was not intentional but Mrs Goodison knew she could never explain it away should Robin find out. Sally was such a treasure. In the months after Robin left home, when the pain was still raw, Sally appeared at her side in the market and suggested a cup of coffee. Their meetings were now a regular occurrence. Mrs Goodison never asked directly, but somewhere in the conversation about everyday trivia, Sally would drop in a few words about Robin, and

Mrs Goodison would depart with a lighter step.

This morning she had not seen either Sally or Robin and, having taken an extra turn round the market with a full bag, she now admitted defeat and set off for the car park and home. George would be wondering where she had got to.

16

Penn sat in the kitchen looking out at the rain, a steaming mug of tea on the table before her. They had planned to go into the dales this morning but in this rain there was no point. She turned as Robin entered, freshly showered after her morning run. "I see you've got your breakfast alright," she said.

"Cold pizza from last night," Penn replied holding up her own slice. "I saved the pepperami and mushroom slices for you."

"Great. I'm starving." Robin opened the fridge and pulled out the bent pizza box. She knew no-one else who shared her taste for this particular morning treat. "I'll be busy all day getting those accounts sorted. What are you going to do? You can borrow the car if you want to go visiting."

Penn looked at Robin, trying to discern the meaning behind the words. "Oh, I don't know, haven't thought about it, really." She still found it hard to know quite where she stood in their relationship. Days, even weeks could pass where they spent all their time together, and then all of a sudden, Robin would do this: create a distance between them by implying their lives were quite separate. "I might just watch the telly. There's an old black and white film on later."

This could often be enough to get Robin to join her, especially if it was a weepy, but not today. "Right, well I'll be up in the spare room. I'll do these later, and dinner tonight, if you like. Can't have you feeling like a housewife, always doing the chores, can we?" Robin placed her used dishes in the sink and left.

The low, leaden-grey clouds outside settled over the town like an oppressive blanket. Penn moved desultorily from room to room, feeling trapped by the weather and her thoughts. Today the house did not feel like her home. Robin's withdrawals disturbed her. They had been lovers for weeks now but Robin still maintained their separate bedrooms. They slept together often enough but always in Penn's room. She never invited Penn into her own bed for the night. They spent hours talking and yet Penn still knew little of Robin's innermost thoughts.

She slumped into a chair. The summer would be over soon and her place at United meant moving to Burnden to live. It was not possible to commute without a car and even then it would be over an hour's drive each way. What was going to happen? She knew her own feelings clearly enough; she wanted to be with Robin. But Robin had indicated no desire for permanency. In fact, she hardly ever touched on the subject of the future and when she did it wasn't their future she talked about. Picking absently at the threads on the arm of the chair, she argued with herself. "*She likes her privacy, you know that. And you don't want to know everything about her anyway, there's nothing wrong with secrets as such. No, but openness about feelings is important. I do need to know. I'm entitled to know. But you don't want to push her away, do you? If you put pressure on her she could withdraw altogether. After all, you don't know everything about her, so how can you know why she behaves like this? But I can't go off to United without knowing how she feels, whether I have a reason to come back.*"

Penn's chest constricted when she thought of not returning, of being without Robin. "*I have to find out, one way or the other. I just have to. I'll do it tonight.*"

True to her word at breakfast, Robin made the evening meal. She was an excellent cook when she did get around to taking charge in the kitchen. Her mood was much more buoyant than it had been that morning and she was full of chat, but Penn kept delaying.

"I got the figures right first time, for once," Robin was saying, "and we're doing better than I thought. Sally's going to be pleased. We might even be able to afford the redecorating she wants in the back room."

"That's great."

"Isn't it? You know when we bought the place I thought Sally was quite mad. I told her it would never take off, that we'd never pull in enough women to break even, never mind make anything on it. Just shows how wrong you can be, doesn't it?"

"Mmmm."

"What's up with you tonight, love? You're not saying much. It's not my cooking is it?" Robin was laughing but concerned.

"No, of course not. It was delicious." Penn managed a smile.

"Well, you didn't eat much of it. What are you worrying about?" Robin did not like to see her this way, so unlike her usual confident self. "It's not that bastard your mum lives with again, is it? You didn't bump into him when you went out, did you?"

"No, no." Penn took a deep breath. "It's about moving to United, I ..."

Robin broke in before she could go any further. "You'll be fine. Jude will look after you, and although it's a much bigger club you'll settle down in no time. And once you start showing them what you can do on the pitch, they'll be all over you. You'll soon make friends."

"Yeah, I suppose." Penn's nerve failed her for the moment and she turned on the TV as a refuge from further conversation.

Robin went up to bed at about eleven. Penn stayed saying she wanted to watch a new comedy show. She went up the stairs half an hour later and got ready for bed, then returned to Robin's first floor bedroom. The light was on, so taking her courage in both hands Penn tapped at the door. "Can I come in?"

Robin looked up and put her book to one side. She'd been half expecting this. She patted the bed beside her. "Sit down."

Penn sat near the foot of the bed, legs crossed facing Robin, her features serious. She twisted the cord of her dressing gown around her fingers, keeping her eyes downcast.

"What is it, love?"

Penn finally looked up, her eyes sombre. "You know training starts again in a week or two, Coach, and I'll have to move to Burnden, don't you?"

Robin nodded. "Yes, you mentioned it earlier, but I had realised myself too." She tried to keep her voice light and easy. She found Penn's presence in the room strangely disorienting, as if some gravitational force had shifted leaving her giddy and off-balance.

"Had you? It doesn't seem to be bothering you that much."

"What d'you mean?" Robin protested, stung by Penn's tone. "Of course it bothers me. I love having you here."

"Do you?" Another question. Robin's disorientation increased. Penn's directness was shifting the established pattern of their life, like turning a kaleidoscope. "Of course I do. Who else would I get to look after the place the way you do?"

"Is that what I am then? A glorified housekeeper, a kept woman, a convenience? Is that all you want from me?" Now it was Robin who looked away from the accusation in Penn's eyes. "Well?"

"No."

"Why do you keep shutting me out then, like this morning?"

In the silence that followed Robin was acutely aware of the thumping of her heart. She wanted the warmth between them back, not this. "Come here, Penn. I can't talk with you away down there." She held out a hand. As Penn moved her gown fell open slightly and Robin felt a sharp tug of desire in her belly. Penn settled at the top of the bed, but to one side and still facing her. "What do you want me to say?"

"It's not what I want, it's what you want to say, that's what matters. I know how I feel about you, but what do you feel about me?" As she voiced the question Penn's heart leapt into her mouth but she did not waver.

Robin picked up Penn's hand twining their fingers together. "I don't know what I'm going to do without you. I don't even like to think about it." She faltered and was dismayed to feel tears pricking behind her eyes. What was this?

"But we need to think about it," Penn pushed Robin harder. "I need to know what to plan for, whether I'll be coming back or not, for instance?"

Robin felt cornered. She was silent, sensing danger and the approach of an invisible boundary she should not cross. She searched for an answer which would not trap her further, but would be truthful. She played for time, "What d'you mean, whether you'll come back? That's ridiculous!"

Penn was losing patience. "Is it?" How clear did she have to make it? Not getting an immediate answer, she looked away. "OK. I'll take that as a negative shall I, Coach? Once I go that's it, it's over." The blood pounded in her ears. But at last she seemed to have got through.

"No!" Robin was appalled. "No, of course not. That's not .... I mean .... I want you here, you know that."

"Wanting me here isn't enough. Why do you want me here? What do I mean to you?"

Robin lay back against the pillows. Dear god, how could she

answer that? What exactly did Penn mean to her? She couldn't even allow her mind to form the necessary words, much less speak them aloud. She felt vulnerable, exposed, but Penn was waiting. "I don't just want you here, love, I mean I want you." Robin emphasised the last word. "Don't you understand? I want you." She was close to breaking point.

Penn relented. "I know you do, I just needed to hear you say it." Seeing her expression she pulled Robin closer. Robin hid her face in Penn's neck but the shudder of her shoulders gave her away. Penn lifted her head with a gentle but insistent finger and saw Robin's eyes brimming with unshed tears. Penn was mortified. "Shh, don't cry, my darling, please, I can't bear it. I didn't mean to upset you, shh now." She cradled Robin against her, rocking and soothing her. A muffled voice came from below her chin. "I'm trying not to."

"Shh now, it's OK." Penn marvelled at this unlooked for reversal of roles, feeling powerful and protective. She stroked the dark head on her shoulder rhythmically for some time, until she sensed Robin was calm. "You're exhausted, poor love. I better leave you to get some sleep." She dropped a tender kiss on Robin's forehead and made to get off the bed.

But Robin did not let her go. She raised a tear-stained face to Penn's. "Stay with me, please. I need you." The admission was a whisper.

"I love you," was Penn's soft response as she put her lips to Robin's.

As their kiss deepened Robin lost all sense of a separate self. Her bones dissolved. She felt an intense need for closeness, to absorb Penn deep within herself, her hands busy removing all the barriers between their bodies.

Robin's touch was arousing Penn almost beyond endurance. She was overtaken by a fierce desire for possession and she moved her hand downwards over Robin's soft brush of dark hair and into the moistness beneath. Robin grunted into her neck, a soft denial of her pleasure. Penn's fingers found the swelling bud hidden under the tender flesh, slipped over and around it. This time Robin's thighs drew apart, her hips lifting slightly in irresistible response. Penn slid her hand further into Robin's wetness.

"No, ooh god, Penn, oh please ..." Penn's entrance was deep and unhesitating, bringing Robin to a mind-shattering climax which left her limp in Penn's embrace.

Recovery was slow. For Penn, secure in the knowledge of Robin's final acceptance of her, there was absolute contentment, evident in the way in which she gradually relaxed into sleep, curled against Robin's side. In contrast, Robin refused the raw intimacy of her experience even while her body shook with the echoes of her insistent pleasure. Already she hungered for a repetition, filled with dread at the vulnerability such profound longing brought with it. And yet. She looked at Penn, sleeping peacefully beside her, and knew with a deep certainty that life would be a dull and dismal business without her. She turned over, careful not to disturb Penn, and lay staring into the dark.

17

Robin rose at first light having hardly shut her eyes. She could not bear Penn's proximity a moment longer. Despite the night's soul-searching she was no nearer knowing how she felt or what to do about it. She slipped quietly out of the bedroom. Maybe a run would help.

As her feet hit the pavement with an unrelenting monotony, her thoughts swung with her arms, first this way, then that. Her limbs still felt the echo of last night's fire. Half her mind urged her to go back and join Penn, to embrace this new self, familiar but strangely incomplete, created in the night. But the more fearful half grew stronger with the passing miles. Only heartache lay in that direction. Best to cut her losses now; she couldn't afford this sort of risk. She needed to remain her own woman, self-contained, inviolate. Dependency brought only disaster. She kept on running.

Penn awoke with a smile ready to greet her lover, filled with deep calm after the emotion of the night. But Robin was not lying beside her and her smile faded. Then she caught the sound of crockery clinking faintly from the kitchen. Relaxing once more, Penn mused how like Robin it was to wake early and go for her usual run even on this special morning. She wriggled down into the duvet, the scent of

Robin's presence bringing a flush to her cheeks. She let herself drift off, only to be woken by Robin's shout.

"Breakfast's ready, Penn."

Wrapping her dressing gown around her, Penn made her way downstairs. Entering the kitchen she moved behind Robin's chair and bent to wrap her arms around her neck, nuzzling into its softness. "Morning, darling," she murmured.

Robin shrugged under Penn's embrace and gave no more than a grunted greeting before returning her attention to the newspaper in her hands.

"What is it, Coach? Has there been some bad news?"

"No more than the usual daily quota. Why?" Robin's tone was flat.

"You seem a bit distant, upset, I don't know."

"Good grief, Penn. Just because I want to read the paper in the morning, instead of mooning over each other. Just give me some space, will you?" Robin's eyes met hers briefly over the top of the paper, devoid of any expression. Penn felt dizzy, she could not breathe.

The rest of the meal was eaten in a silence broken only by the rustle as Robin turned over pages. Penn dragged herself slowly back upstairs to dress. She felt tears pricking at her eyes but did not give way. It would be alright. It had to be alright, she told herself fiercely, *"there'll be a simple explanation, you'll see. Just give her space like she said. Keep out of her way for a few hours."*

"D'you fancy something Italian for supper tonight? I'm just going shopping. I can get whatever you want."

"Get whatever you want. I'm not fussy."

Still, no harm in trying, thought Penn, a while later as she busied herself preparing what she knew to be one of Robin's favourite pasta dishes. She took extra care over the appearance of the table, choosing matching dishes to serve from and placing a couple of candles in the centre. She'd given Robin space, a whole day with hardly a word. Penn leant out the back door and called.

"It'll be about five minutes, if you want to clean up."

Sitting opposite Robin for the meal, Penn watched her carefully, trying to judge her mood. The utter blankness of the morning had gone. The conversation was sporadic, but at least Robin answered, if only in monosyllables.

"Are you feeling better now? Working in the garden always seems to sort you out."

"I didn't need sorting out, thank you," Robin's reply was brusque.

"No, of course. Sorry. I didn't mean anything."

Robin waved her hand at the table and the empty plates. "I suppose this was all for my benefit too, to sort me out, as you seem to think I need." Her tone became sarcastic. "Even candles, how romantic!"

Penn dropped her eyes quickly to hide her pain.

"Well, I'll do the washing up, just to show my appreciation, shall I?" Robin stood and began clearing the dishes as she spoke, removing any thought Penn might have entertained of lingering in the candlelight.

Over the next few days the backbiting became a pattern. Even when Penn tried talking football, the one topic on which conversation from Robin was guaranteed, it made no difference to the distant, often hurtful way Robin responded to her overtures. Penn's features took on a desperate, haunted look. While in public, Robin assumed a false heartiness which failed entirely to deceive Sally, who watched in dismay.

The house developed a chilly atmosphere. The easy repartee of previous days was replaced by terse interchanges, liable to flare into argument over nothing at all. Coming in late one evening, Robin surveyed the kitchen, determined to find fault. "Don't you know yet that this has to be dried immediately or it goes rusty?" she demanded angrily, waving a chopping knife under Penn's nose.

"You used it, you bloody well wash it up!" Penn shouted back. "God! I'll be glad to get out of here, away from your endless nitpicking. You're so bloody unreasonable!"

"It's my fucking house, I'll live as I damned well please," Robin yelled, and so it went on, day after dreary day.

Penn could find no way through. She concentrated bleakly on her preparations for moving nearer to the Burnden United ground, packing her possessions, arranging with Flic, another trainee, for a lift to her new home. Her sole remaining goal was to get out with the remains of her pride intact. Having laid her heart so clearly on her sleeve, she now wanted only to hide its extensive bruising.

The morning of her departure finally arrived. Flic was coming at ten thirty. Penn's bags were at the front door by ten and she wandered restlessly about the rooms. Robin watched her from beneath lowered brows, ostensibly reading the morning paper. Her heart was pounding. She knew her behaviour was unforgivable. The silence stretched between them, the atmosphere taut as a drum.

Several times she tried to summon the courage to explain.

A car horn sounded outside. Penn jumped up. "That'll be Flic. I'll get my stuff into the car." She took her empty mug into the kitchen, then moved briskly through to the front door. Opening it, she called out a greeting to Flic who was waiting by the open boot.

Robin sat, frozen into her chair. *"Say something, do something, for god's sake! You can't just let her walk out without trying."* But she could not find words.

The bags were quickly stowed and the boot closed with a snap. Flic moved to the front of the car and climbed in behind the wheel. Penn came back into the house and stood in the doorway to the hall. Robin stood also and they faced each other, a yard or so apart.

"Guess I won't be needing these any more." Penn held the house-keys in her outstretched hand. Automatically Robin's arm extended and the keys fell into her palm.

"Penn." She took a deep breath but her voice continued to shake. "I ... I'm sorry ... ." Penn regarded her impassively, waiting. Robin's throat closed over. After a further pause, Penn nodded. Then she turned on her heel and was gone.

Robin heard the car drive off, moved uncertainly into the room, looking about her as if she was a stranger there. She picked up the phone, dialled and waited a moment, then hearing Sally's voice at the other end, "Sal ... ." was all she could manage.

"Stay put. I'll be there in five minutes."

And Sally arrived to find her friend sitting on the stairs staring blindly in front of her, tears rolling down her face, her body shaking uncontrollably. Sally sat beside her and held her close. "Oh, Robin, love. I'm so sorry. Let it go now, it's OK. I'm here, love. Sally's here to look after you."

<u>18</u>

Penn looked around the spacious changing rooms. Light came in through the narrow windows along the top left side. Most changing rooms she knew were permanently damp and steamy from the combination of showers and bodies, but not this one. Moving to join Burnden United was certainly a move in an upward direction, no doubt about that. She'd been there only five weeks, but already she felt a sense of familiarity.

Burnden was larger than Deepdale but very similar: there were the hills all round, the industrial heritage of blackened terraced streets and grandiose municipal buildings. The main difference lay in a more prosperous, go-getting atmosphere reflected in a rash of new housing estates spreading outwards all round the town. These embodiments of modern suburbia contrasted strangely with the sombre centre of Burnden with its pillars and semi-circular balustrades, where the echo of a brass band seemed forever just fading into silence. The town's mining history was deeply etched into the character of the buildings which made up its heart. The municipal grandeur quickly gave way to a maze of small terraced streets, one or two still with the cobbles showing through under the tarmac. Then came the more substantial houses on wider roads where well established trees softened the skyline over small open spaces, gardens and parks. Finally, there was the encircling band of new developments, the endless rows of all but identical houses, often smaller than the terraces their occupants were so keen to avoid.

Jack and Darren, the groundsmen, greeted Penn each morning. She was an early riser and often first of the squad to reach the ground. Darren was an easygoing lad, somewhat shy but always eager to please. He passed his days placidly, busy with whatever task he was set. Jack took a shine to her in a grandfatherly way, proffering advice on everything from her passing technique to the need to eat a good breakfast. His favourite topic was how to tackle and his admiration for Penn's ability in this department was great. "Opposition can't do owt wi'out the ball, now, can they?" he would say, nodding his balding head wisely.

Penn's first two games in the reserves went well. During the first, she was responsible for a clearance off the line which kept the scores level and in the second, a three - nil win, she scored the final goal. The other players made her welcome and she was kept busy both on and off the field. One feature of United which she discovered only on joining the club was the rather hectic social life the players shared. Friday night was a pre-match no-go area but other than that it seemed someone held a party every night of the week. Penn, with Flic and Janet, her new flatmates, went along to all of them. She preferred the bustle and noise to spending time in the empty flat with her memories. Her easygoing manner and gift for drawing people out quickly made her popular. One or two players approached Penn seeking more than platonic friendship, but took no offence at her lack of interest. She knew most squad members by name within a couple of weeks.

After her performance in the reserves, Jude called her up as a substitute for the first team in the third game of the season. Not only did she get on the pitch when a colleague pulled a hamstring, but she also had a dream start to her United career when a lucky rebound brought her a winning goal. She tried hard not to let it go to her head. The following week she sat on the subs' bench for an hour before Jude brought her on in a tactical shift. The team were a goal down. Cath, the big centre-forward and top scorer, missed an easy chance or two and the defence were struggling to hold out down the left.

As Penn completed her warm-up stretches she listened to Jude's advice. "Tell Cath I want her to drop deeper and feed off you. I want you to push up on the left midfield and Sarah to switch to the centre. Got that?" Penn nodded. "OK. On you go."

Penn ran on, passing Jude's instructions round the team as she moved across to the far side of the pitch. It was a couple of minutes before she spoke with Cath but the new formation quickly began to work and United players perked up. There was still more than twenty minutes to go, easily enough time to pull a goal back.

With the play focused on the left half of the pitch, Penn was in the thick of it. Several times she picked out Cath with an accurate pass, only to see her waste the chances. She appeared to be having one of those days when nothing went right: either her first touch would let her down or her final shot would be wayward. Cath's temper was not improving as a result. Along with her height of roughly six foot Cath's strength as a forward was her aggressive play, but every now and then it could spill over into outright viciousness. With the close attention the opposing defender was paying her, it looked like tempers were about to fray. When Penn next got the ball she could see Cath's marker was stuck to her like glue, so she moved forward herself, looking for alternative options. Then suddenly she was past the last defender, so she let fly. Shouts of "super-sub" echoed round the ground for several minutes after the ball hit the back of the net. Her elation lasted most of the week.

Now, here she was, back in the changing room amid the hustle and bustle of final preparations as a member of the first-team starting line-up. The other players were encouraging, and offered advice to calm her nerves. "Just keep your concentration, Penn, and you'll do fine," Jude said, drawing the team talk to a close. "Right, now let's get out there and show Hampden Villa what a real team is made of!"

For the first twenty minutes, Penn did not seem to be able to get into the match. The ball was hardly in her part of the field, but she kept her eyes open, absorbing the ebb and flow of the game. It seemed pretty even, but Villa's left side was weaker, she thought. That was why the ball was over the other side of the pitch so much; United were putting pressure on the weak point. Then Villa had a spell of possession and Penn was busy tackling, running, retrieving with no time for further reflection or analysis. She was glad to hear the half-time whistle, then surprised by the comments of her team-mates as they made their way into the changing rooms. She'd forgotten about this being her debut. Jude's half-time talk did not single her out again, but she remained conscious of the warmth and acceptance other players were giving. One in particular, Cath, seemed to be watching her with interest.

By the end of the game, Penn was tired but happy. United won with a late goal by Cath. Penn gave a good solid performance, nothing very spectacular although there were a few saving tackles, but, more importantly, no mistakes. She knew a regular place was within her grasp, a feeling confirmed by Jude's brief comment on her play. She sat back on the bench and let her mind drift a little as the changing room slowly emptied.

Cath sat down beside her, uncomfortably close. She was a solid woman, with broad thighs and blunt shoulders. She rested her hand on her knee, showing off a muscular forearm, and bent her head, with its thick crop of short blond hair forward.

"You've got a lot of power packed into that tight little body, haven't you, love?" Cath said, her lilting voice a surprise, with a soft Welsh accent.

Penn smiled, nodding, not really concentrating. As a result she missed the predatory gleam in Cath's pale blue eyes, failing also to note that they were alone in the room. Cath's arm round her shoulder startled her. Penn looked up, suddenly wary, but too late. "And I bet I could really get your motor running."

Cath's breath was hot on her face and her lips fastened to Penn's, the strong arm holding her firm. "Now, now. Don't be coy." Cath continued, ignoring Penn's struggle. "I'm really hot for you, youngster. I'll give you just what you need." Her hand pushed up under Penn's shirt, searching.

Penn broke away, panting and without thinking her hand flashed out, catching Cath full in the face. "Don't you bloody dare!" she hissed, forcefully. Without another word, she turned and marched out of the changing room, her face flushed, breathing hard. So, again, she missed the expression on Cath's face, this time of venom.

Cath was unused to rejection in any form, never mind this. "Just you wait, bitch, I'll sort you," she vowed under her breath as she rubbed her cheek, her fair skin flaring scarlet from Penn's blow.

19

Robin was pleased with herself. The new season was off to a good start. It took a week or two to re-balance the team into a new format without Penn, but they were well on the way now. Three wins, two draws and a loss left them nicely placed in the table, easily in touch with the leaders but not yet seen as a real threat. The good form of the previous season seemed to be staying with them which was just as well in the stiffer competition of the top division.

Life was good, as long as she didn't let herself drift into memories of the summer. That was over. She'd made a mess of it, she knew, but there was no use crying over spilt milk. Sally, Ingrid and Jude all gave her the same initial sympathy, followed with practical advice: "pick up the pieces, learn the lesson and get on with your life".

The party was in full swing, with Ingrid and Sally taking centre stage. After seventeen years together, they'd suddenly decided a celebration was required. Notices went up in the bar announcing a private party, invitations were sent. Robin, as a present to them, arranged the catering and DJ. Regular customers and friends did the rest and the result was a resounding success. Sally and Ingrid were radiant, their friends delighted. Robin watched them for a few minutes, thinking back over the years, feeling the strength and depth of love she felt for these dear friends. She nodded, smiling to herself.

"And what's brought such a wistful smile to those beautiful lips, may I ask?"

Robin looked round. Beside her was a small, round woman whose curves were emphasised by the soft clinging fabrics she wore. Her face was amiable, and a little worn, with no attempt to hide the signs of age. There was a mischievous sparkle to her eyes as she watched Robin's assessment.

"Well? I think that's two answers you owe me now."

Robin could not help smiling more broadly. "The first one is memories," she replied, "and as for the second, I think I need to know your name at least, before we go any further. I'm Robin."

"Ruth," the woman responded without hesitation. "And before you ask, I knew Ingrid years ago but we'd lost touch until recently. I hadn't met Sally before, but she's lovely isn't she?" Robin agreed wholeheartedly.

"Did you see the bust-up between Cagney and Lacey a few minutes ago?" Ruth asked, and continued as Robin looked at her with a puzzled expression. "You must know who I mean, they're unmistakable." She pointed across the room and Robin laughed as she recognised the two police officers.

"No, I didn't see, tell me about it."

"Well, it was over little Bo-peep, the saleswoman." This time Robin knew immediately that Ruth was referring to Sheila, an incorrigible flirt with a penchant for fluttering her extra-long false eyelashes at all and sundry. "She was making eyes at Cagney while Lacey was buying the drinks, see, and when Lacey turned round Cagney was admiring her earrings a little too closely, so she nudged her, just to get her attention, understand?"

Robin nodded.

"Well, Cagney nudges back, like, what do you think you're doing pal? So Lacey's drink goes over, doesn't it? And where does it go? Right. All over Bo-peep! So she trips off to clean up and doesn't come back. Cagney and Lacey are still arguing about who was in the wrong."

"They've been together a long time. Arguing's a way of life for those two." Robin laughed again at the accuracy of Ruth's nicknames. "From what you say, I gather you don't go for the Bo-peep style?"

"No. I like my women with no artificial attachments."

"What none, not ever, in any circumstances?" asked Robin with a wicked lift to one eyebrow. "I find some attachments can have their attractions, in the right situation."

"Do tell. I can't imagine what you mean." Ruth called her bluff, her eyes wide with mock innocence. "Maybe you'd care to demonstrate?" A laugh bubbled in her voice and Robin felt a familiar thrill run through her. She was surprised at her own interest. Ruth was very different from the young women who usually caught her attention.

Ruth continued her exploration of the probable occupations of other women filling the bar, from solicitor to street-sweeper, bag lady to boardroom executive. She finished with a devastating analysis of a woman in the property business. Then her voice took on a challenging note, "Of course, I had you pegged for a quantity surveyor, right from the start."

Robin frowned slightly as she tried to guess what would come next.

"How about you tell me the result of that valuation you carried out on me earlier?"

Robin grinned, the woman's audacity was appealing. "Mmmm," she paused, savouring the suspense, noting Ruth's breathing had shallowed. "I think about forty, fully matured in the nicest way, of course, and well-cushioned against the harsher side of life," this was said with an appreciative glance over Ruth's full hips. Then, as Ruth's satisfaction showed clearly in her eyes, she added in a more intimate tone. "Sure of what you want, not afraid to take it, altogether an expert in giving and receiving pleasure."

Ruth moved deliberately closer so that her breasts just barely touched against Robin. "You're a bit of an expert yourself, when it comes to pleasure, aren't you, Robin?" She made her voice a little huskier, but the knowing gleam in her eyes was undimmed. "No qualms about taking it where you find it, I guess."

"I've always found I can get what I need," Robin agreed. "There's always something to please a roving eye." She indicated the bar, thronged with women of all shapes, sizes and shades. She moved her leg, putting Ruth a little off balance, causing her to lean more heavily against her. One arm dropped down and fixed round Ruth's ample waist. Ruth laughed again, shaking back her tightly curled bob of hair.

"Very practised," she said appreciatively, taking full advantage of the opportunity to lean against Robin. "So strong, aren't you. I'm tempted to faint away just so you can pick me up again. How about you whirl me round the dance floor instead?"

They moved into the edge of the crowd. Ruth, like many ample women, was light on her feet with an excellent sense of rhythm. They danced through several records, never more than a few inches apart. Ruth was a skilled and sensual dancer, Robin quickly found, flowing around her partner, mirroring and leading, weaving an intricate pattern, but without ever touching.

In a brief pause between records, Ruth said lightly, "I think we could go somewhere a bit quieter now," and taking Robin's hand led her off the dance floor. Sally caught Robin's eye as she went towards the door and raised a quizzical eyebrow. Robin gave the faintest of shrugs and grinned.

Robin found it a novel experience to be taken charge of in the way Ruth was doing, but it was not unpleasant. Part of her mind was still on the dance floor, savouring the mobility of Ruth's body and her own response to it. She felt no impatience. There could be no doubt about what would happen next. Neither of them said much, content to allow the sexual undercurrent of the early evening to build up silently.

She followed Ruth to her car. It was a only matter of minutes before they drew up in front of an old warehouse building, now converted into smart apartments. Once again, Ruth led the way.

They were soon in a room with dimmed lights, muted music and a glass of chilled wine. Robin sat at ease on a large settee. Ruth was beside her, leaning sideways, one leg tucked under her, her arm along the back of the settee, fingers meandering through Robin's short hair. Her other hand rolled the cold glass against her slightly flushed cheek. Robin was stirred by the contrast of pale palms against the darker skin of Ruth's face.

"Still waters run deep." The quiet comment caused Robin to look up. The wicked gleam in Ruth's eyes deepened and she smiled before continuing. "It's alright. I don't want to know why. I prefer my mysteries unsolved. It's less complicated that way." Her fingers pulled softly at Robin's earlobe. "And you are a mystery, Robin, there's no doubt of that, a mixture of cool detachment and raw sexual power. It's a combination that really excites me."

Robin dropped her gaze for a moment. Ruth was nothing if not direct, it seemed.

"So just how excited can you get," she asked, the teasing tone back in her voice, "and what do I do to make you succumb to this sexual power of mine?"

The answer was not a verbal one. Ruth opened her eyes wide, her lips parted as her tongue flicked out to moisten them. She reached up, recaptured both Robin's hands and pulled her forward. In the same movement Ruth slipped down and under Robin's body so that she lay beneath her, soft and yielding. Robin could not refuse the invitation.

She was not sure what caused the change. Certainly it wasn't lack of responsiveness on Ruth's part. Robin felt separated from what was happening. Even while she continued the physical activity of lovemaking, she became disengaged, her body withdrew from Ruth's caresses, even as Ruth's response reached its crescendo. Ruth neither commented nor pressed her, allowing Robin to hope that she remained unaware. They lay for some time in a quiet soothing embrace.

In the car outside Robin's house Ruth touched her arm gently. "Thank you Robin," she said. "I needed someone tonight, more than you could know, and you were more than I hoped for. You're a real treasure. Don't be too hard on yourself, will you?" She just smiled at Robin's startled look, urging her gently out into the night.

Robin made her way slowly up to her bed. It wasn't as late as she'd thought but an uneasy feeling remained as she thought back over the night.

20

The bus lurched around the corner hitting the kerb with a sharp bump which nearly threw Penn onto the floor. Even now, she had to check twice to be sure this was the right stop; even when she'd lived here with her mother and Stan, she'd found it hard to tell the streets and houses apart. She pressed the bell on the ceiling and moved down through the packed bus to get off. Although she had rung beforehand to be sure she would not encounter her stepfather, she was still slightly nervous as she walked up to the door. There was always that small chance that he could be home after all.

It had been a struggle to bring herself to visit her mother again. In the end it was Flic and Janet who persuaded her to try to patch things up. They were sitting in the flat on a weekday evening picking over the remains of an Indian take-away. Janet began to talk about her family and how she wished she lived nearer to their Tyneside home. She twisted her fingers into her shoulder length mouse-brown hair, absently biting the ends as she reminisced about family nights in with her numerous brothers and sisters.

"I'd think you'd have been glad to escape a madhouse like that," Flic teased, always the joker among the three of them. She and Janet were of similar height and build but there the likeness ended. Janet's mousy colouring went along with a quiet, reflective temperament, perhaps well suited to the stresses of goalkeeping but she was finding it hard to settle. Flic's extrovert personality led to other difficulties. On the football pitch, she suffered from her impetuous behaviour; enthusiasm led her into frequent debates with referees. Off the field, she was just as quick to speak before thinking. The red hair which many people thought explained her impulsiveness was not natural, as her brown eyes demonstrated to those who looked more carefully. "Anyway, it's not your family you miss at all, it's that hunky boyfriend you never let us see."

The blush was quick to rise under Janet's cheek. For distraction, she turned to Penn. "You live really close to home but you've hardly gone back at all, why not?" And Penn found herself explaining her estrangement from her mother and why they only spoke on the phone.

"That's a real bastard you've got there, Penn," said Flic, shocked into seriousness for once. "I'm not surprised you don't want to go back, but don't you ever worry about what could be happening to your mum?"

"I do," Penn agreed, "but I don't think he's ever hit her or anything. He better not." Her fists clenched in her lap.

Flic added "I remember in some documentary I watched where they said that if a bloke was violent it nearly always got worse, not better." She stopped abruptly as she saw the colour leave Penn's face.

Janet shot Flic a look of annoyance. "Shut up, you idiot! Of course she worries, but saying stuff like that isn't going to help any, is it?" Janet took Penn's hand in hers. "You say you get on quite well now on the phone, yes?" Penn nodded. "Well, why don't you arrange to meet up somewhere? Then you could see for yourself that she's fine."

Penn was doubtful at first but as Janet and Flic talked it through with her she agreed to find out her mother's reaction. It had been much more positive than she expected. Her mother had suggested they met in the town centre and, over several cups of coffee, Penn began to realise just how much she missed her mother's company. The abuse was still strictly taboo. However, her mother said "You know, Stan's still mad about pub quizzes, he's even joined some league or other. Means he's out every Thursday night. I get to catch up on all my soaps, just so long as I remember to set the video!" Penn laughed at this reminder of her mother's obsession. "Maybe you could come and join me sometime?"

This invitation was added quite casually. Penn had agreed in just the same tone, and now here she was for an evening of soap opera heaven. Mrs Nibbs (Penn had understandably kept her father's name when her mother remarried) was not a passive observer of television, more a passionate participant. For Penn the enjoyment was not in what happened in the soaps but in her mother's outspoken biases in favour of one character over another. She muttered, scolded or encouraged her way through the programmes, adding her own spice to the dialogue. She was a seasoned fan and nothing was guaranteed to get her going as much as when she felt someone was being made to act out of character. She would become quite incensed with the stupidity of scriptwriters who didn't know their duty to the public or to the history of the plot.

"What d'you keep checking the time for?" her mother asked with an edge of irritation, for despite her enjoyment, Penn kept a watchful eye on the clock.

"I just want to be sure I catch the bus OK," Penn replied easily, although her real concern was to be out of the house and away before her stepfather came home. Her mother's attention was already refocused on the TV screen.

"For goodness sake, you fool, she's taking you for a ride, can't you see? She's only after you for one thing, and it isn't your body!" This comment was directed to the handsome face of a middle-aged man in the process of succumbing to the best-known golddigger in the community.

Penn took the cups and plates they'd used through into the small kitchen and washed up. She wondered what her mother would say if she had to explain the dirty dishes. But then, her stepfather probably didn't notice anyway. It felt good to be pottering about here again and she was surprised by how easily she and her mother had fallen back into old habits. Wishing that the foundations of this renewed relationship were more solid, she put the dishes back in their accustomed places and hung the tea-towel over the radiator to dry.

Returning to the front room she picked up her coat. "I'll be off then, mum. I'll give you a call when it looks like I can get over again. It's going to be a bit hectic with the international trials coming up, but I'll try."

"Just whenever you can manage," her mother replied, ignoring the reference to football, as usual. "Go on now, out of my way before the adverts finish." With a quick hug she saw Penn off at the door and returned immediately to the television.

21

There was a real buzz in the changing room, more than usual for a cup-tie, even in the All Leagues. The opposition today was Burnden United and so far the Town was holding them to a draw. The girls were full of talk, with frequent references to one United player in particular: Penn, of course. Every one of them noticed how her game had improved. She'd gained in strength as a benefit of more frequent training, but the main development was in her uncanny ability to read the game. It was clear she was a lynch-pin in United's game plan despite her recent arrival in the team. The Town players were unstinting in their praise, even though it was Penn who was giving them most trouble.

Whatever the result today, Robin thought, this game was a godsend. The attendance was the biggest Town crowd in ages, many of them coming to see the "old girl" duo of Penn and Jude. Town supporters maintained their loyalty over long periods, following departed stars as eagerly as the current team. There was also no mistaking the boost her team got from holding out for the first half. Robin found it hard to bring them down to earth in the short half-time team talk, but she didn't want to break their spirit with too many reminders. After all miracles did happen in cup- ties, almost on an annual basis. A draw certainly seemed a possibility.

Even watching Penn was a delight rather than a strain. Robin was proud of Penn's progress, now a regular in the first team and obviously fulfilling her early promise. Robin made a mental note to check in with Jude after the game, she must be really pleased. Unsure of her reaction to Penn, Robin had avoided the arrival of the United bus and so missed her usual chat with the opposition coach in the executive suite.

She followed the team out and was soon absorbed in the game, shouting encouragement and instructions from the sideline. United didn't break through until the eightieth minute, and, inevitably, Penn was the architect of Town's downfall. She threaded a beautifully weighted pass through the Town defence, catching Phil unawares. There was a mad scramble in the six-yard box and the ball came flying out again. Before Robin could express her relief, Penn's left foot flew up in a high overhead arch, connected sweetly with the ball and sent it rocketing back into the goal. Josie hadn't a chance. The crowd went wild, their double allegiance never clearer.

Robin was still savouring the goal when the whistle went and the teams began to file past her towards the showers.

"That was a scorcher," she said as Penn came up beside her. "Have you no pity, doing that to your old team-mates?"

Penn grinned that familiar dimpled grin, her delight showing all over her face. "It was a close run thing, Coach. I had to do something to show I can still learn you Town players a trick or two." Then she was past and gone.

Robin had a brief word with the team, singling out Steph, Carol and Mandy for praise, and agreeing with them all several times that, yes, Penn's goal would take some beating for goal of the season. She left the changing room and climbed the stairs to the bar where she knew Jude would be happily knocking back the beer.

"She's a jewel, isn't she?" Jude was ecstatic. "What a player! You know she's been called up for the England squad, don't you?" Then she suddenly remembered the events of the summer. "Sorry, Rob, probably the last person you want to talk about. I forgot for a minute there."

"It's OK. I'm over that now." Robin shrugged, then smiled at her old friend. "And I have to agree with you, she is a cracker! I'd be delighted to see her in an England shirt." Robin paused. "When am I going to get my reward for sending her your way? I could have persuaded her to go anywhere, you know."

"I'm eternally grateful, Rob, old pal. I can't afford what Penn's worth to United, not with all the other outstanding debts I owe you. But I can buy you a beer." Quickly the two of them fell to reminiscing, reliving their own cup triumphs and tragedies before getting down to a detailed analysis of the afternoon's match. It was one of the rare days when they agreed on that, too.

22

Penn looked around her feeling more than a little overawed by what she saw. Spread out around the training ground were between twenty and thirty of the top players in English women's football, bending and stretching their way through the preliminary warm-ups. Already she had spotted several of her heroines; Mandy Barker, Sue Fletcher, Ally Bowyer and Chris Black were all here. These women had all been in the team that made it through to the semi-final of the World Cup only three years before. Penn pinched herself surreptitiously. It surely couldn't be true that she was really here with a chance of being selected for England when she'd only been at United for a few short months.

The appointment of a new manager for the national team appeared to have resulted in a sweep of the proverbial new broom when it came to picking the players. More experienced women had been passed over in favour of fresh talent. The bulk of this new, experimental squad called up for trials were in their early twenties and completely untested at international level. It was an enormous gamble for the manager to take, but Penn, herself, felt less conspicuous in this crowd of newcomers. A couple of others were there from the United team, which meant at least some familiar faces to draw support from.

Brenda Trafford, the new manager, blew her whistle to catch the players' attention and issued a series of instructions. Soon Penn was fully occupied with testing her ball skills against one of the other new recruits, dribbling and tackling back and forth along a twenty yard stretch of the pitch. Then they were reformed into foursomes to concentrate on passing, first along the ground, then including half-volleys and heading. All the time, Brenda urged them to aim for one touch passing, picking out those she saw using three or more touches for comment. Penn was the recipient of such remarks more often than she would have liked.

It wasn't until well into the five-a-side knockabouts that it dawned on Penn that the word trial was a misnomer. They were all of them part of the squad, it was just a question of who would be selected to play in the matches. The thought made her miss the ball completely, ending up flat on her backside. As she stood up amid the laughter, she thought ruefully, *"Well, it won't be me, then, will it? Not unless I prove I can actually kick the ball."* The training continued in a similar manner, ending with the finale of a friendly full scale match with half the squad on each side.

At the end of the day, Brenda gathered the women together again. "You all know why you're here" she began, "but some of you are new to the peculiarities of international football. You may be expecting a decision about your call up now, but I'm afraid that's not how it works. I can't judge you properly on a single day's play. No sensible manager would dream of using that as a basis for an international selection. The fact that you are here at all is part of your answer, and what you do between now and the next international date, next month, will provide the rest of it. Today was about getting to know each other. It was for me to see how you play best together, and to work out possible combinations. Obviously I have some ideas." Brenda grinned at the shuffle of expectation which occurred among the younger women in front of her. "But I cannot finalise anything at this point in time. Let me reaffirm, you are all now members of the England international squad." There was a collective sigh. Brenda raised her hands. "So much can happen in a month, injury, loss of form, even, god forbid, suspension for ill-discipline. The team will be announced as close to the game as possible, which also gives us the maximum tactical advantage. You'd expect no less from any decent manager, now, would you?"

The faces around her were serious and attentive. "We don't have time for another full training session before the next match against Wales, but don't go thinking that means I'm not watching you. I am. As I've said, today I've formed some ideas, but they aren't set in concrete and each of you can affect my final decisions. Think about all that we've done today. Show me that you are worthy of it and you'll get the chance to wear that England shirt you want."

With those final words, Brenda dismissed them to climb aboard the coaches which were waiting to return them to their respective grounds. Penn travelled home to Burnden with her emotions swinging from elation to despair. She was in with a chance despite her mediocre performance in the training, but could she prove herself worthy?

23

It was Flic who saw the article first. She picked up her copy of *OUTfield*, the lesbian sports monthly, on her way home from work. Flic was still playing in the reserve "B" team so she put in a few hours a week at the local superstore to help her finances. Neither she nor Janet begrudged Penn's success, and the living arrangement suited them all. She didn't want it to change, so her first thought was to worry that Penn would be moving out to stay with one of the girlfriends mentioned under the cover-page title: "Lesbian soccer sex: the inside story on life with rising star Penn Millard."

As she skimmed through it, Flic realised the story was a fantasy. Nothing of the Penn she knew appeared in the article, except for the pictures and they were given misleading captions. She recognised most of the women featured with Penn and knew that none of them were lovers. They were mainly hangers-on from the many United parties. The only accurate bit in the whole shebang was the fact that Penn was a rising star. Penn must be laughing up her sleeve, Flic thought, getting paid to have this rubbish printed. She left the magazine on the hall table, meaning to rib Penn about it at the first opportunity.

"How much did you sting them for, Penn?" Flic asked as she came into the sitting room later that evening. "I can't believe they swallowed that rubbish."

Penn's face was uncomprehending. "What are you talking about? What rubbish? How much did I sting who for?"

"Come on, you know what I mean. In this month's *OUTfield*," Flic persisted.

"What is?"

Slowly it dawned on Flic that Penn's puzzlement was real. "My god, it wasn't you. Then I wonder what cheeky sod ... Hang on I'll get it for you, you'll die laughing." Flic retrieved the magazine from the hall and passed it to Penn.

Penn's reaction was not laughter. Far from it. "Shit! It makes me out to be some kind of sex fiend!" She swore loudly and colourfully, using language Flic did not think she knew. As she read on through the article, Penn's face grew darker. "Bloody hell! I'll strangle whatever bastard made up this crap." She waved the magazine under Flic's nose. "Did you read it?" When Flic admitted she hadn't read it properly, Penn continued, quoting.

"Listen to this, "Penn Millard may be a rising star but is she rising under her own steam or is somebody pulling her upwards? Football is well-known as a hotbed of sex and intrigue. Who's to say she isn't getting a leg up (or even one over)." Shit, they might as well just say I'm sleeping my way to the top. Who writes this trash, and where did they get the pictures?"

Flic, and Janet when she came in, did their best to reassure Penn, saying most people would treat it as a joke, especially anyone who knew her. This led to renewed distress from Penn. "How can I go into the changing room after this, nobody'll even look at me."

"It's not about you, Penn. It's clear to anyone this has been made up from nothing. Ignore it. Laugh at it. Anything, just don't let it get to you. It's not worth it." Janet's voice was urgent. "You're a brilliant player, Penn, no-one doubts that. They'll all be focused on what you do on the pitch. Most of them couldn't give a toss what goes on anywhere else. You could be getting your international debut in a few day's time. Think about that."

But Penn continued to seethe inwardly. She knew this was no coincidence. Someone had deliberately given this crap to the magazine and persuaded them to publish it.

24

Tuesday evening came, and with it the international, England versus Wales. While this fixture never had quite the edge of an England - Scotland contest there was, nevertheless, a lot of pride at stake. Both national teams had their fervent, and committed, supporters whose rival voices were echoing around the stadium. To the left, were the ranks of red and blue with a generous fluttering of Union Jacks declaring for England. On the right, a mass of green and yellow seasoned with liberal amounts of leek, daffodil and dragon could not be mistaken for anything other than the Welsh contingent. Undoubtedly there were some neutrals here and there but this was a night for partisans.

The noise rose to a thundering roar as the two teams ran out, looking suddenly puny on the vast expanse of the pitch. The grass was patterned into diamonds by the mower, bands of darker and paler green alternating out to each corner. The formalities completed, the players scattered around the field for their last few minutes warm-up before the whistle. The Welsh voices swelled stronger after the boost of winning the mini-contest of the anthem. There was no mistaking the passion with which "Land of my Fathers" had resounded from the stands.

The England captain made her last round of the team, joking with the few experienced players, reassuring the more nervous newly-capped youngsters, bringing their minds to focus on the game about to begin. In the opposite half, the Welsh captain urged her team-mates to give no quarter in the tackles, to run every extra yard willingly and, above all, not to stop until they heard a whistle. In contrast to England, the Welsh were a team of seasoned campaigners. "Let's get at them right from the off," she commanded. "They're a bunch of babies. If we rattle them early they'll never get into the game."

Two other United players were in the England team but despite this reassuring familiarity Penn could not relax or bring her thoughts to focus on the huge importance of the occasion. Her mind kept wandering. There had been a few ribald remarks from her team-mates as a consequence of her unwanted fame, but Penn tried hard to follow her friends' advice and react with humour. She barely managed it, but it did put the others off. She'd been surprised to make the team, fearing the *OUTfield* article would have counted as evidence of ill-discipline, but Brenda Trafford, at least, had made no mention of it.

Her jangling nerves were not improved when Brenda announced that there'd be one-to-one marking for this match. That meant she'd be facing Cath all evening. Cath didn't like her; since that incident in the shower, they'd hardly exchanged a word except that Cath had been the first to comment openly on her alleged position as the siren of women's football. Penn did not relish the prospect of ninety minutes close proximity. It was a tough job marking Cath at the best of times; she was up to every trick in the book.

For the first time in her life, Penn was not enjoying a football game. It was a scrappy game, with no form. None of the players were settling. The ball spent a lot of time in the air, always a bad sign, but Penn was glad. In the general mediocrity, her own lack of form might go unnoticed.

The crowd grew restless as neither side managed to capitalise on the mistakes made by the other. The songs and chants became less raucous and then less frequent. An atmosphere of frustration and dissatisfaction began to form, quickly communicating itself to the players and unsettling them further. There was a brief return to the happy anticipation of the kick-off when the Welsh left winger made an inspired dribble from deep in her own half, but the final cross was over-hit. England did not manage even one coherent move in the whole of the first half. One look at the manager's face as she made her way down to the dressing room told Penn it would not be a happy interval.

The second half began well for England with a spell of sustained pressure. Suddenly they were passing the ball with confidence. The Welsh defenders were scurrying to and fro, chasing the ball and not watching the players. England forced three corners in a row, and now the crowd were on their feet again. Ally Bowyer bent to place the ball on the corner angle, raising her left hand in a wide arc as she did so.

To most of the team this meant little, but Mandy Barker recognised the signal. She moved imperceptibly back, away from the crowded penalty area, out to the edge of the box. Then as Ally moved to strike the ball, Mandy made her run. Fast and strong she came through the jostling players aiming for the spot she knew the ball would pass, level with the far corner of the six-yard box, just as Ally had signalled. Her head met the speeding ball with force, sending it angling down past the outstretched hand of the Welsh keeper. Then the rest of the team were surrounding her, ecstatic in their joy.

But the Welsh came back with renewed vigour, urged to still greater efforts by their own fans, who once more drowned out the English. The balance of the match turned again as the green and yellow shirts surged forward in numbers. Cath was large and menacing as ever in the centre-forward position.

Penn, as the tension of the match reached her legs, was struggling to cope with Cath's size and speed. Every time Cath got by her, she taunted her, "come on short-arse" or "where's your legs". Penn gritted her teeth, she knew better than to rise to such bait. The Welsh pressure continued, and as they battled Cath's remarks became more personal, "nobody lit your fire today, darling?", and "who were you busy with all night, then?" Penn was losing control of her temper and Cath could sense it.

They were jostling for position, ready for a free-kick to Wales. Cath kept up a constant murmur. "Thought you could take a short cut, didn't you now, with that glamour puss act? Bit of a flash in the pan, you'll be all washed up by Christmas without anyone to take care of you. Why don't you leave the game to us real women? It's not for little lover-girls like you. Save your talents for the bedroom, that's what you're good at, isn't it?"

Penn shoved at Cath angrily, nostrils flaring, "Shut up!" But it went on. "Got a temper, have we?" Cath leered, "Don't go getting excited now. This is the football field remember, not the boss' bedroom." She spun away as the cross came over, but Penn was quicker, thumping the ball out for a corner. It brought no release. It wasn't the ball she wanted to hit. Cath was back at her ear. "Nice little system you've got, haven't you?" she sneered.

The winger took the corner, low to the edge of the box. Yet again Cath and Penn fought over the ball, Cath using her height and weight unfairly, digging her elbow into Penn's neck. "Please the boss in bed and you think you can have anything." Penn snapped. She forgot the ball, forgot the rest of the team and the watching crowd. She concentrated on Cath, landing several blows to her stomach and one to her chin which knocked her over onto her backside.

Then it was over. Arms were pulling her off, voices were telling her to calm down and suddenly there was the referee. Penn looked her straight in the eye, offering no excuses, and followed her direction to leave the field for an early shower. As she stomped off, still raging, the last thing she saw was Cath's gloating smile.

25

Robin looked up enquiringly at the knock to see Phil standing in the doorway to her office looking a little sheepish. "Have you got a moment?"

"Sure, come on in. What is it?"

Phil cleared her throat, a blush rising to her cheek. "D'you remember I had a week or so off a couple of months ago?" Robin nodded, "Yeah, stomach bug or something wasn't it? Are you feeling bad again?"

"Not exactly." Phil took a deep breath. "It wasn't a stomach bug. Chris and I were trying for a baby. We thought we'd made it, then I had a really heavy period which might have been a miscarriage. It shook me up a bit."

"Phil, why on earth didn't you say? Bloody hell!" Robin ran her hand through her hair trying to remember how sympathetic she'd been. She asked gently, "It's happened again?"

"Yes. I mean, no!" Phil grinned as Robin raised her brows in puzzlement. "I mean, no, that hasn't happened again but yes, I'm pregnant." Another deep breath. "It's just, well, Chris and I both think I shouldn't be playing any more, you know, just in case."

"That's great news, Phil. Congratulations! I'm delighted. I can see why you think that way, but what the hell are we going to do without you?"

A blush rose under Phil's dark cheek. "I know. It's really short notice, but I don't want to take any risks. And anyway I'd be no use most days, I've been pretty sick." The note of pride was unmistakable and Robin swallowed a grimace. It was getting more common but deliberately choosing to become a lesbian parent was not something she'd ever contemplated for herself.

"You poor thing, it must be horrible," Robin sympathised, but her mind was already racing ahead. "Go on now. You get back to Chris. She'll be wanting to look after you already, knowing her." She waved Phil away, with an admonishment not to forget them all entirely.

Robin was pleased for her, but it left her with a problem. There was no-one else with Phil's obvious authority in the side. She'd have to try a few of them out, but that meant disruption, uncertainty and tension for the next few games. This wasn't the best point in the season to be making changes. The run-up to the Christmas break always sorted out the real contenders from the also-rans. They needed to secure three wins out of five games if they were to have a chance, Robin reckoned. She drew patterns on the paper in front of her as her mind ran over the different possibilities and team formations.

Carol came through the door and Robin looked up. "Did you hear about Penn?" Carol was obviously shocked and Robin's first thought was for injury. Her heart jumped into her throat; surely not now, right at the start of her international career. That was too cruel.

"What about her?"

"I just can't believe it." Carol continued, "I mean she was always so calm and controlled. She never let anyone get to her, not even when a saint would retaliate. And this was one of her United team-mates."

"What happened?" Robin asked again. The match was on the television in the executive suite, courtesy of the inter-club network used by all the clubs for coaching. Most of the team was up there to watch. Robin had meant to join them but was delayed when Phil dropped the bombshell about leaving. She hadn't noticed the time.

"Sent off. She went berserk. There's no other way to describe it. Honestly, her fists were flying. She really laid into Cath, knocked her right off her feet, and Cath's no pushover."

"What? Penn?" Robin's disbelief was clear.

"Yes. Penn. Nice quiet little Penn." Carol shook her head grimly. "It really hasn't been her week at all, what with that thing in *OUTfield* too." At Robin's renewed puzzlement, Carol gave her the gist of the article. "Come up to the bar, I've got a copy up there. It's a real dirty piece."

Robin agreed. It was gutter journalism. She was surprised. *OUTfield* was a serious magazine not given to this sort of rubbish. There was little about football in the piece, little of any substance, but plenty of innuendo and suggestion. It wasn't a fair reflection of the game, but even more it was a totally distorted picture of Penn and her talent. Anyone with half an eye could see that Penn's talent was real, she had no need of any "leg up". Penn might well have another lover by now, but she didn't believe for a minute this trumped up story of girls all over the place. Bed-hopping was not Penn's style at all.

The more she thought about the article that night, the angrier she became, and the more she felt other emotions resurfacing. Ones which she thought dead and buried. It was unbearable to think of Penn suffering like this. Robin was sure that the article and her outburst on the field were connected. She hoped Penn's friends were standing by her. She'd be needing all the support they could give.

26

Passing through the changing room, Jude studied Penn out of the corner of her eye. She'd seen the outburst during the international a few days earlier, finding it as shocking as anyone. She did not understand what Cath could have done to provoke such a fiery response. Penn was a strong-minded woman but, until Tuesday evening, Jude would have sworn she was even-tempered and the last player to be tempted into wild retaliation.

Cath, when Jude spoke to her that morning, seemed just as bewildered. "I've no idea, Jude. It was just an ordinary tussle, then, all of a sudden, she's flying at me." Cath shook her head, her pale eyes wide, and shrugged. "She hasn't spoken to me since."

Penn was withdrawn but otherwise appeared to be alright. Jude went on into her office. She hoped Cath would be able to sort it all out. She'd promised to try and talk to Penn during the training session. Jude's policy was to allow the players to have first go at dealing with these sorts of disputes. She only intervened when nothing else produced results. This was partly because she hated emotional entanglements, partly because it usually worked. She had a funny feeling this was more complicated than it looked and her heart was heavy as she turned to the paperwork in front of her.

Out on the pitch, Penn concentrated on the training routine, familiar from long practice. She tried hard to empty her mind and allow the physical exertion to soothe her. She didn't speak much, only when addressed directly. Most of the team, after a careful look, left her to it, sensitive enough to know now was not the time to offer condolences or support.

As they trooped back into the changing room, glad to get out of the drizzle, there was obvious surprise when Cath was seen drawing closer to Penn. Imperceptibly, the other players moved ahead faster, leaving the two of them to a semblance of privacy. It was like Cath to grasp the nettle like this but no one wanted to stay around and be stung.

Cath blocked the corridor, forcing Penn to a halt. "I think we need to do some straight talking, you and I." Her voice was low and threatening.

"I've got nothing to say." Penn spat out the words without looking up.

"Oh, but I have, you jumped-up little squirt." Cath, using her size to her advantage, backed Penn against the wall, leaning with one hand over each shoulder. Penn was effectively her prisoner. "So you better listen." Penn resigned herself, biting her lip in frustration.

"You think you're god's gift to football, don't you? A few lucky miss-kicks and you're the new star of Burnden United." Cath's tone was brutally sarcastic. "Well, if you want to stay here, there's only one way to do it. It's me you have to please, not Jude. She only took you on out of sympathy for that Goodison woman. They were thick as thieves for years 'til they split. And I know how you got in the first team so quickly. Just can't keep your knickers on, can you, when dropping them for the right woman will get you what you want? Well, OK. That's your business, but if you want to stay here you better share that sweet, busy little cunt with me." At Penn's horrified look, Cath laughed deep in her throat, leaning closer. "It's that, my little spit-fire, or a permanent place in the reserves. Even a transfer can be arranged."

Cath was so sure of herself that her hands were already dropping down to Penn's shorts and her pupil's were dilating as she leered lustfully into Penn's face. Penn's response took only a split-second.

"I wouldn't piss on you if you were burning," she hissed. With a well aimed punch under Cath's diaphragm, Penn had the satisfaction of taking the wind right out of her sails before she walked steadily away.

Penn went straight to Jude's office, ignoring the other players as she passed through the room. Shutting the door behind her, she spoke quickly, before she lost her courage. "I can't play here any more."

Jude swung her chair round and stared at Penn's determined expression. Her eyes were over-bright and her cheeks flaring red, but her gaze did not drop from Jude's.

"Sit down, Penn." Jude motioned her to a chair. "Take a few deep breaths, calm yourself down, then tell me what you mean by that." She waited as Penn sat.

"I can't play here any more. I want a transfer," Penn said again.

"Penn, I know you've had a hard week. First the international with all the debut nerves. Then the shock of a sending off, which by the way we need to talk about, but there's no reason to think that means you've got to leave United." Jude ploughed on, despite the stony expression which remained on Penn's face. "You're a good player, Penn, with time and hard work you could be a great one. Don't throw it all away because of a silly mistake. I know Cath doesn't bear a grudge. She's a generous woman, Penn. Talk to her, apologise, and you'll find everything's OK again."

For a third time, Penn repeated her request. Jude began to get exasperated with her. "You can't just come in here and demand a transfer, Penn. That's not the way it works. For a start you're still on a training place at the moment, not a contract."

"OK then. I resign. Am I allowed to do that?" Penn's tone was insolent.

Jude tried again to get her to explain. "Look, Penn, this is ridiculous. Tell me what it's all about and we can work something out, but you're a member of this squad until I say otherwise, understood?"

Penn shrugged. "I'm not going to play and I won't be training either." Her voice was low and sullen but the set of her chin signalled the determination within.

"OK. That's it! If you won't talk to me about it, I have no option. For the last time, Penn, tell me what's behind this, or, never mind resigning, I'll suspend you as from this very minute."

Penn remained stubbornly silent. Jude, feeling backed into a corner, nevertheless followed through on her words. "Right. Pack your gear and go home. I don't want to see you here until you're ready to talk sense. Out. Now!"

27

Robin pushed her chair back from the table and patted her belly. "That was delicious. I'm absolutely stuffed." As usual Ingrid's cooking was of a high standard. "You're wasted in the bar. We should do something about adding a restaurant."

It was an old refrain of Robin's and Ingrid smiled. They'd been round this track several times over the years. She could never quite get Robin to give up on the idea, despite her protestations that she only enjoyed cooking as a pastime.

The three women took up their accustomed roles, proceeding to clear the table and wash the dishes. Robin always took her stand at the sink, Sally dried and Ingrid put away. It was a routine established years before and came as easily as breathing. In no time, the evidence of the meal disappeared and they relaxed in front of the fire with a brandy and coffee each. The first weekend of every month would always find them here, in the flat over the bar. Conversation flowed back and forth, as they discussed the refurbishment of the back room adjoining the bar, and preliminary plans for the Christmas party, before Sally brought up the subject which really interested her. Ingrid could not suppress a smile. She knew Sally was dying to ask about the night of the party. She was surprised she'd managed to hold back so long.

"So-oo," Sally drew the word out. "Spill the beans then. What was your first experience with an older woman like? Did you like her?"

Robin's eyebrows rose as she and Ingrid exchanged glances. "That's a beer I think you owe me. It took more than an hour this time." Ingrid nodded, chuckling at Sally's scowl. They both knew how annoyed Sally was when they bet on her curiosity in this way.

"She was a lovely woman," Robin admitted. "Warm, responsive, mature and undemanding. Yes, I liked her."

"But ..." Sally quizzed.

"It's as if I've shut down or something." Robin spoke after a long silence. "I don't know what's the matter with me. I just didn't feel anything really, and Ruth's a nice woman. I really did like her." Both Sally and Ingrid could hear the distress in her voice.

"How d'you mean, love?" Sally's enquiry was gentle. She knew the soft centre which lay within Robin's cool exterior, how fragile the protective facade really was and how difficult she found it to deal with powerful emotions. Ingrid rose quietly and went out to the bathroom and Sally blessed her silently for her tact.

A slight colour rose under Robin's cheeks. "I mean nothing happened for me. It was sort of, mechanical, going through the motions." Her voice was low. "I don't usually have any problem that way." Her eyes flickered up to meet Sally's and then away again.

Sally made an encouraging sound and Robin went on haltingly. "It was all fine here in the bar. I was enjoying flirting with her. She's a real mover on the dance floor. But then, when we got down to it, later, I just dried up. I don't think she minded, she got what she wanted anyway. I could still manage that at least." A wry grin crossed Robin's features.

"Maybe it's just a bit soon," Sally offered. "After all, you were pretty cut up over Penn, weren't you, love?"

Robin nodded, still unsure. "Perhaps, but I've seen her a few times since, what with the cup game and stuff. I feel alright about that, honestly I do." She emphasised the last words as Sally frowned slightly.

"It's probably just a matter of time. Don't worry about it, just concentrate on having fun. You'll be OK, I know you, the proverbial rubber ball. You just got a bit more squashed than you're used to." Sally's words seemed to cheer Robin.

Ingrid returned. "That bathroom desperately needs replastering. It's getting worse beneath the window. You know Sally, we're going to have to do something about it."

"I know, love, but we haven't got a lot to spare just now."

Robin made a suggestion which she knew Sally would resist. "What about taking some of the profit from the bar this year? It's done really well, and if you got it done at the same time as the work in the back room, I'm sure it'd make hardly any difference to the bill." Ingrid looked pleased, Sally less so. "Go on, Sal. You've hardly taken anything out of the business the last two years. You're owed it."

"At least think about it, love, it really does need attention soon." Ingrid joined in.

"OK, I'll think about it, but no more than that." Sally tried to look stern - and failed.

Later that night, as they were getting ready for bed, Sally confessed her concern to Ingrid. "It's taking her a long time to get over Penn. And it's not just Penn either. I think this goes deeper. There's something eating at her but she doesn't know what. I'm worried about her."

"I know you are, love. Any one with a problem or heartache and you're there, ever-ready with a shoulder to lean on." Ingrid's loving look took the sting from her words. "Good, solid, dependable Sally. Everyone talks to you. I could get quite jealous if I didn't know better." This remark was accompanied by a kiss on the tip of Sally's nose. "Robin's going to be OK. She's got more strength than you give her credit for. She's a survivor, isn't she?"

What worried Sally was the cost of that survival.

28

United were doing well and Jude didn't want that to change. She racked her brains for a way out of the impasse. If only she could have got Penn to talk. Cath told her she'd tried but got nowhere, and Penn remained stubbornly silent. It was disrupting the whole team; the other players were puzzled by her continued absence. Not only was Penn popular, but she was a key player in most of their tactical planning.

The one figure who kept coming to mind was Robin. For one thing she'd been Penn's coach at Deepdale Town, for another Jude knew from her own experience that Robin had a knack of providing support while women worked out their own troubles. The big drawback was the affair of the summer. But that was some months ago now, she reflected, and Robin had said herself that it was past history. She just couldn't think of anyone else to try and after two weeks' stalemate she had to do something.

Jude reached for the phone and dialled. As always Robin was pleased to hear from her. They chatted for a few minutes before she came to the point.

"I need a favour, Rob." Jude was the only one who shortened Robin's name in this way. It was a habit established years before during the very brief affair that had started their friendship.

"Anything I can do, you know that, Jude. You only have to ask."

"Well, don't say that before you know what it is," Jude cautioned. "I know it's a bit of a cheek and I'm trading on your good nature more than usual. But I just don't see any other option."

"You must be in a right pickle if I'm the best you can find," Robin chuckled. "Not pregnant are you?"

"No." The smile in Jude's voice was replaced by a more serious note. As she continued, she felt a similar change in Robin. "It's about Penn. You know she got sent off?"

"Mmmm."

"Well, it seems to have thrown her right off balance. Cath's tried twice to talk to her about it, and got nowhere. She won't say a word to me, except that she wants a transfer or to tell me she's resigning. I can't get anything else out of her. I ended up suspending her, she drove me so mad." Jude's frustration was still obvious in her tone.

"My god! She really got to you, didn't she?" Robin was surprised. Jude was not a stern disciplinarian on the whole.

"I shouldn't have done it, it hasn't helped any. I still can't get any sense out of her. I even went round to the flat but she virtually ignored me. I'm at my wit's end, but I can't let her back until she apologises at the very least."

"She can be stubborn, but she's not usually totally blind to reason. Didn't she say anything about what's behind it?"

"Not a bloody word. That's why I'm asking you. It's not really fair to, after what happened in the summer, but I still think she might listen to you; and she's certainly not listening to anyone else. She's too good a player to lose, Rob. We need her. Is there any chance you can have a talk with her?"

Robin drew a long breath. "I don't know," she replied, then making up her mind, "but I can give it a try. It's only fair to give her a chance to explain. I know she'll have been upset because of that piece in *OUTfield* too. Maybe it's got something to do with that."

Jude had missed the article, but when Robin described it to her she became even more convinced that she'd made the right decision in asking her old friend. "You can talk to her about that, Robin, you know how that feels. She'll listen to you. I wish I'd seen that myself," she added. "Maybe I'd have managed things better if I had."

After agreeing to come over to the United ground the following lunchtime, Robin hung up in a thoughtful mood. There was something that didn't quite add up. She was pretty sure she was right about the article being at the root of the trouble, but why had it led to the outburst against Cath?

Her mind went back over the years, analysing how she'd felt when Lucy's bombshell hit the newsstands. She'd been hellishly angry, it was true, ready to lash out at anyone and ashamed that such intimate details of her life were spread out for public view. Penn would feel much the same, she knew that. Perhaps Cath had said something insensitive. If Lucy had stayed around to say anything, it was possible that Robin could have lost control; but Lucy had vanished like a puff of smoke. As a result, what Robin never found out was Lucy's side of the story.

Lucy had leapt at the chance to write for a national daily when she met the editor of the paper's sports page at a social do she'd attended with Robin. Lucy took the editor's word that she wanted a serious article covering the contribution of lesbians to the success of women's football. She'd written her piece, without telling Robin for fear of interference; and sent it in good faith. She had not written, and was horrified by, the sensationalist piece of trash which appeared in the next edition under her name, nor were the photographs hers. She'd rung the paper only to find herself alternately fobbed off with waffle about the editor's rights, and congratulated for producing such a scoop. She knew what Robin's reaction would be and could not face it. So she left, taking her shame and Robin's trust with her.

It was while Robin was washing the car that another realisation struck her, so forcibly that she didn't notice the hose spraying her shoes. Thinking about Lucy was something she rarely did. She buried the episode deep down in her mind, refusing to confront any of the pain directly.

They'd been inseparable. Robin, deeply in love for the first time, had held back on nothing. She shared it all with Lucy, her hopes and fears, her most secret dreams for the future. And her body, utterly and without reservation.

Suddenly noticing how cold her feet were, she looked down. "Oh, bugger it!" She dropped the hose and moved to turn off the tap. The car was clean enough. As she went in the back door, sat and removed her shoes and socks and dried her feet, Robin's thoughts were still in the past. Lucy's betrayal hurt her deeply, but not 'til now did she realise where the scar was most sensitive. Not since Lucy, had she let herself become truly intimate with anyone, either physically or emotionally. Not until Penn. The truth stared her in the face. She'd punished Penn for Lucy's treachery all those years before. It even explained her experience with Ruth, she thought bitterly.

As she dried between her toes she admonished herself fiercely. *"You've got some growing up to do, girl. For someone thirty years old, you ought to have dealt with this emotional baggage long ago."* She better take care not to let Penn bear the brunt of any other emotional scars if she was to be any help to her, she thought.

29

Robin, having misjudged the amount of traffic, arrived early at United for the lunchtime appointment. She made use of the spare time by getting Jude to show her round the impressive facilities. Jude's office, in contrast to Robin's cramped, basement cubicle, looked out over the pitch. The other training facilities were also on the ground floor. Apart from the airy, spacious dressing room with its sparkling new showers, there was a gym and a weight-training room, and, best of all, instant access to the club physiotherapist.

Jude confirmed that Penn was to meet her in the office, so they returned there and chatted while they waited. When Penn arrived, Robin was shocked by the change in her appearance. She slouched into the room. Her posture implied she had no right to be there, that she wished she was invisible. Her skin was sallow and there were deep shadows under her eyes. The reason for Jude's level of concern was now unmistakable.

There was an awkward lopsided conversation for a few minutes with Penn's contribution minimal and grudging. Robin, seeing how embarrassed both Penn and Jude were, took control.

"I hear there's a really good pizza place in town, and I'm starving. Let's go, if you're ready, Penn?"

She kept up a one-sided conversation until they were settled in the booth with a large pizza between them. Penn was relaxing slowly, but she wasn't giving anything away. Robin decided upon a direct approach.

"What was it, Penn? Did Cath say something about that stupid article?"

Penn munched doggedly on a slice of pizza. "Did you read it?"

"Yeah, I read it. It was an appalling piece of trash, but anyone who knows you would see it had little to do with you. I wrote to the editor complaining about it. I think you could sue them for libel if you wanted." It was true Robin had written a letter the day after reading the piece.

"It wouldn't make any difference if I did. Whoever wrote it will be well pleased. I don't have a reputation left to damage since Tuesday." It was the first direct reference to the sending off incident that she had made, and Robin did not let the opportunity go.

"Anyone can lose their temper, Penn. I got sent off three times in one season. What got you so riled up?"

Penn looked across the table. Robin saw the hurt in her eyes, but was dismayed to see fear lurking there too. She resisted a strong impulse to reach out and soothe away the lines on her forehead. "She said stuff." Penn's voice was gruff.

"About the article?"

"Yeah."

Robin waited. When Penn said no more, she continued, "What did she say that upset you so much?" Her voice was warm and full of concern.

Penn shook her head. "It was just stupid stuff. I can't see the point of repeating it."

Robin pressed her further but seeing Penn's agitation increase again, she backed off. Instead she turned her attention to entertainment, bringing Penn up to date with news about the Town players, in particular Phil's pregnancy. Penn was by no means cheerful when she dropped her home, but her step was a little lighter. They parted amicably enough. Penn even agreed to an unspecified future meeting.

Robin reported back, "Sorry, Jude, I couldn't get to the bottom of it today. She agreed to meet up again, and I think she'll spill the beans eventually. There's certainly something serious bothering her. Can you give me a bit longer?"

"I don't suppose I've got any choice, really," Jude replied reluctantly.

"I know it's a bit of a cheek, but d'you think you could let her back in, at least to use the training facilities, in the meantime? She needs to have something to keep her occupied."

"Perhaps," Jude was still thoughtful. "It might be possible, so long as she trains alone and not with the team. I don't want to confuse the rest of them any further with this mess, but I'll talk to her about that. Thanks, Rob. Get back to me as soon as you can won't you?"

30

Late November and early December were slack times in the bar, a pre-Christmas lull before the rush of boozing and parties began. Evenings were slower and more evenly paced, a time to take notice of customers' opinions and suggestions. The plans to renovate the back room as a non-smoking area had arisen this way. Robin had developed a knack of tuning in to conversations without being noticed. She found it generally useful, not just in the bar, but in the changing room, too.

There were a couple of large-ish groups in tonight, it being a Friday, and Robin's attention was caught when she noticed Cath at the centre of one. Each time she made the rounds to collect the glasses, Robin paused a little, near to Cath's group, but the talk was innocuous. It was almost closing time when she heard Penn mentioned. She waited, apparently busy with cleaning nearby tables.

"That was a cracking piece you wrote last month." Cath directed her comment at a new arrival, then turned to the rest of the group. "She had an article in *OUTfield*. Did you read it, girls?"

Some of the women nodded, others looked blank. "You mean the one about mud-wrestling?" one of them enquired.

"No, but I liked the pictures in that too!" Cath's laugh was suggestive. Another voice chimed in, "You mean the one about sex and football, don't you, Cath?"

"Yeah, that's the one," Cath grinned lewdly. "I'm always interested in that."

Robin moved quietly from one table to another taking care to keep within hearing distance of the group. The discussion remained general for a few moments, before the article was mentioned again.

"I was surprised by it. I didn't think Penn Millard needed to do that sort of thing. She's a good player, anyone can see that."

"Don't say you've been taken in by her, too." Cath's voice was hard. "She's a flash in the pan. She only got where she was by sleeping around. She's just like the piece says. Anyone can get in her pants just as long as they're someone in football. I should know." Another leer and a knowing wink accompanied the last statement. "And she's not so hot in that direction either. I've had better." Cath led the laughter which followed.

Robin was deeply shocked, as much by the revelation of Cath's poisonous character as by what she'd said about Penn. Only her quick reactions saved her from breaking a glass she'd nearly dropped when Cath implied she had been Penn's lover.

"I'll get the photos back to you as soon as I can. That was what convinced them to run the story, you know." The stranger smiled conspiratorially at Cath.

31

Robin, busy with an away fixture on the Saturday, went to Jude's in Burnden early on Sunday morning and explained the situation to her. "I never realised what a venomous woman Cath is, but you should have heard the things she said, Jude, and not just about Penn."

Jude was horrified to think she'd only added to Penn's difficulties. "I knew there was something more to it, Rob, you know I did, but it was easier to let them try and sort it out, and I never imagined ... "

"It's your ostrich tendency, Jude. You see things coming but you hope they'll go away, instead of taking action."

Jude wanted to find Penn and apologise immediately; but Robin thought a more cautious strategy would be better and offered to act as ambassador.

"I'll go round to the flat, now, and see if she's in. The sooner we get this properly sorted the sooner she'll be back on the pitch where she belongs."

Penn was a little startled at finding Robin on her doorstep at that time in the morning. "Oh. Hullo, Coach. Um ... come in ... I was just making a coffee. Would you like one?" Robin nodded and followed Penn inside, noting her unbrushed hair and crumpled clothes. She'd look better after Robin shared her news, she hoped.

Penn placed a mug of coffee in front of Robin and, mumbling something about having a bad night, went off into the back of the flat. She returned after several minutes looking freshly scrubbed and a little more respectably dressed. "You're coming out for some fresh air," Robin stated. "Blow some of the cobwebs away. You don't have a choice, Penn," she added, as Penn began an instinctive refusal. "Coach's orders and that's that." Penn subsided, her resistance reduced to muttering. "Who is my bloody Coach? That's what I need to know. I've got you and Jude on my case now."

It was a grey day with scudding low cloud and a freshening breeze. The hills were out, Robin decided, the cloud would be down on the tops closing them in. She turned the car west towards the coast. A good stretch along the beach would do nicely. She didn't speak much, concentrating on weaving the car in and out of the motorway traffic, then down the narrow lanes to the spot of coastline she had in mind. Penn was quiet beside her.

"See that breakwater?" Penn nodded. "I'll beat you there and back," Robin challenged. "Ready, steady, go."

It was a good half mile to the low line of timbers stretching out into the Irish sea. The sand, exposed by the receding tide, was firm but still tiring to run on. Robin managed to keep up with Penn until the last couple of hundred yards, when Penn put on a spurt and left her trailing. Robin drew level with their starting mark, stopped and bent over for a moment, catching her breath. Penn's breathing was deep but even.

"Glad to see you haven't been letting your fitness slide while you've been off."

"You weren't so far behind me, Coach. Not bad for an oldie like you." Penn grinned shyly and ducked as Robin made as if to hit her. "Less of the old, thank you." Robin turned and began to stroll along the beach in the opposite direction to their run. Penn fell in step beside her. The wind whipped around them swirling up the beach and rustling the grass in the dunes.

"Cath was in the bar last night." Robin looked sideways, seeing Penn stiffen. "I overheard a few things which might interest you," she continued. "She's not got a very high opinion of you, has she? Do you know why that would be?"

"The feeling's mutual," Penn returned. "I don't give a damn what she thinks of me."

"She's a dangerous woman to make an enemy of, I'd say. Why don't you like her?"

"She's a crude-minded bully," Penn said. "But everyone at United thinks the sun shines out of her arse. She's cock of the walk there." There was bitterness in her young voice. Penn bent to pick up a stone from the sand, hurling it forcefully towards the distant water. "They won't hear a word against her."

"Try me instead, I'm an outsider."

Penn walked on a few steps before saying, "Not really. You're a friend of Jude's, aren't you."

"You're not telling me she's a crude-minded bully, too?" Robin spoke carefully, keeping her voice free of inflection. "Yes, she's a friend, a good one, but this is in confidence Penn. It won't go further. Jude may have asked me to talk to you, but I'm not her spy and she knows it."

They were standing still now, having arrived at a small inlet where the wide beach narrowed and a stream ran into the sea. Penn scuffed at the sand with her foot, thinking hard. She decided to take the risk. She squatted on her heels, concentrating on building a small pile of stones.

"You were right the other day. She said stuff about me she'd read in that bloody article. She kept going on, getting more and more crude and personal. She said Jude only took me into United because you and she used to be "thick as thieves", that's how she put it. Then she said I got into the first team by sleeping with the boss. I couldn't help it. I just lost my temper and went for her. I deserved the sending off, I know."

"But why did she pick on you rather than anyone else?"

Penn sighed and began to dismantle her stack of pebbles, throwing each one deliberately into the stream. "She fancied me, right from when I first got to United. I ignored her, then after my first full game for the team, she made a pass at me. I wasn't thinking or expecting it. She wouldn't take no for an answer. I just reacted and hit her."

"You seem to be making a habit of that. No wonder she doesn't like you." She couldn't keep the amusement out of her voice and Penn looked at her sharply.

"It's no joke!" she protested. "She even tried to blackmail me."

Robin was aghast. "You're not serious, Penn. That's awful."

"It was, she makes my flesh creep. She got me in the corridor after training. Had me pinned against the wall. She said if I wanted to stay at United then I better let her screw me too, along with the boss. And it was clear she meant Jude, implying I only kept my place in the team that way. She said if I didn't oblige she'd make sure I had no career in football. Seems she was right about that too, the filthy scheming bitch." Penn's voice shook with vehemence. "That's when I went and told Jude I couldn't play any more. She just told me to talk to Cath, as if she was the nicest woman in the world. I knew it was hopeless then, so I didn't say any more."

"It's not hopeless, Penn. It's one hell of a mess, but it's not hopeless."

"It is," Penn insisted. "Only old Jack, the groundsman, will talk to me these days, and I don't see him much as I'm only there at odd times. Cath's probably told everyone I screw him too if she's seen him speak to me. I hardly see the rest of them; they've obviously had instructions to keep their distance." Penn threw the last pebble viciously into the water, then sank her sandy fingers deep into her hair.

Robin squatted down beside Penn and pulled her hands out of her hair, keeping hold of them as she spoke. "You're right about Cath, she is a scheming bitch, worse than even you think. You know she planted that whole story through a contact at *OUTfield*? I heard them discussing it in the bar. She's a really nasty piece of work." Penn's face showed disbelief, then deepening anger. Her mouth opened, then shut again.

"I went and saw Jude this morning before I came to get you," Robin went on. "I can see why you didn't want to say anything to her, but she honestly had no idea what Cath's really like. She was mortified after I told her, thinking of what she'd said, how she'd told you to talk to Cath. She's really sorry, but she'll tell you that herself. If you'll let her."

Robin stood up again, stretching her long legs and wrapping her arms round herself. The wind was cold, and they'd been still for some time. "Let's get back to the car, I'm getting cold." Penn, also suddenly shivering, fell in step again and they walked slowly back across the sand.

After a while Robin spoke. "I know it's hard, Penn. I've been where you are. I had my life splashed all over the daily papers not long after I started with the Town. I know what it feels like, thinking everyone's chewing over intimate details about you. It makes no difference whether they're true or false. It hurts like hell. I wanted to run and hide. Football was my life but I just wanted out."

Penn swallowed hard. "I don't know how I can face them again." Tears were not far off. "That piece made me out to be a promiscuous little tart."

"I know," Robin looked away. "But it's true what they say about fifteen minutes of fame, Penn. Everyone else will have forgotten all about it by now. You remember it because it's about you, but everyone else moves on to whatever the next day's news is. They'll forget the whole thing soon."

"Not with Cath around they won't."

"Jude may not be the most observant of women, Penn, but if there's one thing she can't stand it's a bully. I think you'll find Cath will disappear in a little while, without a trace being left behind. In fact I'd bet my life on it." Penn still looked doubtful. "Trust me. Jude and I go back a long way. That's one thing Cath got right, about us being thick as thieves. I can guarantee there'll be no trouble from her again."

They reached the car and were glad to get in, out of the wind. The drive home was as quiet as on the way out. They pulled up once more outside Penn's flat and Robin turned off the engine. There was one last thing she wanted to be sure of. She looked Penn straight in the eye. "Don't let this come between you and the game, Penn. You're a talented player with a great future. One sending off isn't going to affect that. Most people don't know a thing about all this other stuff and they never will. Get back on the pitch and let your football do the talking. Just go in and see Jude tomorrow and get yourself back into the team. Promise me you'll talk to her at least?"

"OK."

"Good. Well, I'll see you when I see you then. Chin up."

Penn got out of the car and then leant back in through the open door. "Thanks, Coach. I really mean it. I was beginning to think no-one would ever listen."

Robin held up her hand, palm forward and waved away the gratitude, smiling. Then as Penn shut the door, she turned the ignition key and drove off into the dusk of the winter's evening.

32

On Sundays, Jude usually left her players to their own devices so Cath was surprised to receive a summons to the coach's office. She made her way through the building, musing on the possible reason but never suspecting it would be a negative one. She was confident of her value to United. She knocked on Jude's door and walked right in.

"Ah, Cath. Thanks for coming in so promptly. See anyone else on your way in?" Jude's question was not quite casual, and her face relaxed when Cath shook her head in the negative.

"What's with all the cloak and dagger stuff, Jude? What's so secret?" Cath joked, her smile wide. "Some big transfer deal, or what?" She laughed.

Jude took a deep breath. "Actually you're not far off the mark, Cath." Jude ran a hand over her head as Cath's face became serious. "You know we keep getting enquiries from Stamford Rangers about you, don't you?"

"Yeah, sure. But I don't want to move. I'm very happy here, Jude. You know that, so what's going on?" Cath reacted characteristically, becoming instantly aggressive when the conversation took an unwanted direction.

"I think this time we'll be accepting their offer, Cath." Jude's statement fell into a stunned silence. She held Cath's gaze as her words sank in.

"Hang on a minute," Cath blustered. "Who says we will? Don't I get a say in the matter? And what about the board, I'm sure they wouldn't agree. I'm one of the fans' favourites."

Jude broke into the gathering outburst. "That's most likely because they don't know you very well, though, isn't it? If they knew the sort of dirty tricks you got up to, they might change their minds." It was Cath's turn to interrupt, her temper flaring. "Don't be daft, dirty tricks my arse! OK, so I'm competitive, but football's a competitive game. You have to use all the advantages available. You should know that as a coach! The fans expect me to use a few dirty tricks, as you call them."

"Not against your own team-mate, and not away from the football pitch, they don't." Jude's voice was soft but every word was clear. She watched impassively as Cath's face registered shock, then a brief flash of cunning, and finally outraged innocence. "What the hell d'you mean? That's a hell of an accusation, Jude. You better take that back or I'll be making a formal complaint. What the hell makes you think you can stand there accusing me of god knows what without a shred of evidence?"

"Ah yes, evidence." Jude still spoke softly. Only those unfortunate few who ever saw her this angry knew that her voice diminished rather than grew in direct relation to the depth of her anger. "You see I have that too, but not the sort you'd want me to go public with I think." Cath's bluster subsided quickly as Jude outlined the evidence Robin had brought to her attention. "Now, I'm not interested in your motives, I don't even want to think about them to be frank, so don't try and make excuses." Jude's sharp gesture cut Cath off before she could speak. "I don't want the club's reputation damaged by this kind of grimy business," Jude continued, "and I have to admit you've given us good service on the pitch over the years, so I'm prepared to let you off the hook a little. Everyone knows we get requests for your services. They also know that we could do with the boost to our finances. OK they'll be surprised that we let such an asset go, but that's football for you. Managers make stupid decisions everyday." A brief smile crossed Jude's face before she became deadly serious. "But mark my words, Cath, I'll be watching you and if I catch even the slightest whiff of anything to do with this, I won't let the club's reputation stop me from acting."

Cath knew when she was beaten, when to retire from the battle to regroup for the rest of the war. She acted meek and apologetic. She asked about the details of the transfer deal, satisfied to hear that Stamford Rangers were willing to pay a significant sum to secure her contract. She could build a new power base from there and her time would come. Jude couldn't protect the Millard brat forever. As she worked to mollify Jude, Cath's brain was already running ahead, working out the best way to work this deal to her own advantage.

33

Jack's face broke into a wide smile when Penn came into the ground the next day. "How are you, petal? I've been watching for you. Not like you to miss training. Hope you're not sick or nothin'. They can't do wi'out you for long, young lady." Penn smiled back, stopping briefly to chat before braving Jude in her office. She'd come in early to avoid the other players, but she guessed Jude would be there.

She knocked at the door and Jude looked up. "Ah, Penn." Jude continued without hesitation, "I'm glad you've come in. I want to apologise for my insensitivity. I never really gave you an opening, did I?" Her face was penitent and Penn saw the apology was from the heart.

"I suppose not, but I owe you too. I didn't wait long and I didn't offer anything for you to go on. I'm sorry."

Again Jude came straight to the point. "I've had a word with Cath. We've both agreed that a transfer is desirable. There are always clubs interested in her services, and I've accepted an offer from Stamford Rangers, so I don't anticipate she'll be around for much longer. That'll be public news from this morning so there's no need to keep it to yourself. She won't be in the team before going, either, in case that worries you. She pulled a hamstring in Saturday's game, it's not serious but it will do as an excuse, something of a happy coincidence, I think. I'd like her to apologise directly to you, but I understand if you don't feel like seeing her."

Jude waited while Penn thought this idea over. "I'm not sure," she said finally. "Can I give it a day or two to chew on, please?"

"No problem." Jude became business-like. "I gather from Robin that you haven't let your fitness slip. She said something about you running down the beach like a whippet. Nevertheless, I want you to take care today. Nothing too strenuous. It's an important game on Saturday and I'd like you in the team. Show me what you can do in the reserves on Thursday night and we'll go from there. OK?"

Her team-mates were pleased to see Penn back among them. No-one mentioned the magazine although she did see one or two glances pass between them. Penny, who played on the other side of midfield and had several full Scottish international caps broke the ice over the sending off. "Let me have a bit of warning when England play Scotland, will you, Penn? I can make sure I'm positioned well away from you when the excitement goes to your head again."

Penn found Robin's words were true. It was not long before the whole incident seemed forgotten and life returned to normal. The news of Cath's transfer soon fuelled the fires of the gossips with fresh material. She thought hard about Jude's suggestion that Cath be made to apologise directly, deciding, on balance, that it was important to have an opportunity to put the record straight. She asked Jude to arrange the meeting for after the reserve match, and to stay to hear what was said. Jude agreed.

The reserve match was a joy for Penn. It felt good to be back on the football field. There was no feeling to match the one that came with scoring a goal. Her feet certainly spoke tonight, she reflected, as she walked through the corridor from the changing room to Jude's office. She took a deep breath before opening the door and facing Cath.

Penn stood firm while Cath mumbled a half-hearted apology. "I'm sorry about what happened."

"I didn't quite catch that." Penn's voice was clear, untroubled. Cath repeated her apology, louder but without much more conviction. Jude was quiet, staying to one side.

"I don't think it just happened, do you? You'll need to do better than that."

Cath looked trapped, but Penn was adamant. "Look I'm sorry for what happened on the pitch, right. Will that do?"

"But it didn't just happen, did it?" Penn waited again.

"OK. OK. So I'm sorry I said a few things to annoy you! Alright? Is that what you want?"

Penn shook her head. "Not quite good enough. Who was the journalist you persuaded to write the article?" Penn inquired. "I'd like her name, please, so I can pass it on to her boss and make sure I get a full retraction printed next month."

"How do you ...?" Cath's face was a picture. "I can't tell you that, it wasn't her fault. It could get her into trouble."

"That's not my worry, she should have thought about that before she got mixed up with you. The name, please."

Cath turned to Jude for help and found none. Jude had told her, while they were waiting for Penn, that it had been her suggestion that Penn demand a direct apology, but she'd said nothing about any other demands. "Rebecca Drummond," she said, inwardly seething but outwardly subdued. Mentally she added Jude to the list of those with whom she would one day get even.

"And finally," Penn finished, "I'd like you to repeat what you said about me and "the boss" while Jude's here, so that it won't come up again."

She was pleased to see that Cath was appalled by this demand, and the flicker of a smile cross Jude's face. There was a brief silence before Cath, recognising another defeat, did as she was asked. "I said you only kept your place in the team through sleeping with the boss. It was a lie."

Penn moved towards the door. "That's that, then. Enjoy your new club. I look forward to playing against you." She left, feeling extremely pleased with herself.

Jude called Robin, almost as soon as Cath, too, had left her office. "She was magnificent. Stood there haughty as any princess, and just dictated her terms. It was a complete surrender on Cath's part. She's got some guts, hasn't she?"

34

Christmas was just under two weeks away. Robin sat beside Sally in the crowded cafe. They were in town to organise extra bar staff for the Christmas party. After their coffee they would go round the shops to find a present for Ingrid. This excursion was an annual event.

"Where are you dragging me off to first, then?" Robin pretended disinterest but enjoyed the time together as much as Sally did. She already had one purchase nestling at her feet. It was a book for Penn.

She knew it was foolish but something had made her buy it. Luckily, Sally had not asked to see what was in the bag.

"There's a new boutique up on the corner of the square. I thought we'd try it. I'm looking for a shirt, brightly coloured. Something different." Already uncertainty hovered in Sally's voice.

"OK then. Let's be off."

As they left the shop, Robin turned to speak to Sally and accidentally bumped into a woman. Her ready apology froze on her lips as she recognised her mother. She stood with her mouth open, gawping. Her mother was more socially polished, as always.

"Why, Sally! How nice to see you. And you too, of course, dear. It's been quite a while."

Still unable to think of a coherent response, especially in the face of such an understatement, Robin was grateful for Sally's assistance in taking up the conversation. She did not really hear what was said until she caught her name again.

"I was just saying to Sally, Robin dear, that it's so lucky I've bumped into you like this. There was some post for you at the house the other day, probably cards I would think but it might be something important. I was going to post it on to you, but I won't need to now. Sally says you were just going so you'll be able to follow me home and pick it up yourself."

"But, I thought you wanted me to come with you to that new boutique." Robin's eyes pleaded with Sally, only to see the faintest shake of her head.

"No, no. I'll be fine. You go on and pick up your letters. If I don't get anything today we can always try again later in the week."

"Alright then, Robin dear. Now I've just got to pop in to Humphries' for a bit of bacon for your father's breakfast and then I'll be on my way. So if we say twenty minutes. Then we can have a cup of tea and a bit of a chat." With this, her mother walked off and Robin was left with no escape.

"Sal! How could you? I haven't been home in years!" Robin was horrified, but Sally was unrepentant.

"Exactly! And every time I try and persuade you to go, you find some feeble reason not to. Now you have to face up to them." She softened a little. "They're your parents, Robin, they're not going to eat you alive. Just give them a chance. They're good people and they love you. You're too hard on them."

"But Sally, you know what they said about me."

"Yes, I know, love, but you've never given them the opportunity to take it back or say anything else, have you? Be honest, now." She squeezed Robin's arm, secretly delighted at how easily she had engineered the long-delayed face-to-face reunion of Robin and her parents. "Come on, Robin. If they do repeat it, you can just leave, but they won't."

Robin looked uncertain, but walked slowly to the car park. Automatically she got in behind the wheel. She drove with only half her mind on the traffic. Her journey took her out along the main road north and into a neighbourhood of 1930s housing which nestled into a recess on the hillside. Left, left again, third on the right and second left. The old familiar rhythm of the trip led her inexorably to her parental home.

Her stomach gave a wobble as she turned into the road where her parents lived, where she'd grown up. Unconsciously her eye ran over the landscape behind the house, tracing the impression of a huddled giant's figure in the shapes of the hills that her father had showed her so many years ago. She caught a whiff of her mother's scent in the air, although it had to be imaginary. She was still fifty yards from the front door. The last meeting with her parents had been their brief visit to the hospital after she broke her ankle and it was even longer since she'd called at the house. She parked the car and walked up to the door. Waiting, after ringing the bell, she noticed that her knees were trembling, the muscles jumping crazily. Her stomach churned again as she saw her mother's familiar outline through the glass of the door.

"Hello, Mum." She did not know what else to say.

"Come in, my dear, come in." Robin followed her mother along the passage, feeling disoriented. Her mother was behaving as if it were weeks, not years since they had exchanged more than a few words.

"George, dear, look who's here. It's Robin come to see us. Isn't that lovely?" Robin's father sat as he always had, in the chair to the left of the fireplace. He looked up, taking his pipe out of his mouth. "Well, girl," he said. "Well." He put his pipe back in his mouth and clenched his teeth, regarding her somewhat blankly. This was more what Robin expected. Her father had never said much.

"Hello, Dad. How are you?" It was a formal greeting but it felt like the right thing to say. He moved his head to one side, taking the pipe out again.

"Could be better, could be worse." Robin had to smile. She knew that was his stock response and she was amazed at how good it was to hear him say it again.

"Mum said there was some post for me. I've just come to pick it up."

"That's right, dear, now where did I put it?" Her mother riffled through a pile on the sideboard and pulled out two or three envelopes. "Here we are. But you'll stay for a cup of tea, dear, won't you? I've got some mince pies fresh from this morning. I know how you like them."

Again Robin could not refuse the invitation. As her mother moved into the kitchen Robin said, "Can I give you a hand, Mum?"

"Oh, no dear, you stay and talk to your father. I'll only be a minute. Still just one sugar, is it?"

"Yes, thanks."

Robin and her father looked at each other across the hearth. It was easy to see where Robin got her physical appearance. While she had her mother's quick movements and curving mouth, her father had provided her broad shoulders and direct gaze. He was tall too, although it was less apparent when he was seated. He sucked on his pipe for a while, then took it out once more. "Been a while, girl, quite a while."

Robin was unsure how to take this, thinking it signally failed to express the truth. "Well, I've been busy with this and that. The coaching takes a lot of time." She felt an overwhelming desire to giggle but recognised it for the hysteria it was and resisted.

"Mmmm. I see the team's been doing quite well. Won something last year didn't you?" Her father clamped the pipe back in his mouth as if he felt he'd said too much. Robin told him about the triumphs of the previous season and the hopes for this one. Her mother brought in the tea while she was talking and sat by the window as she always did, where she could get a good view of the street.

"These are delicious, Mum. I wish I could bake like you. You always get the pastry so light." Robin was sincere and her mother smiled.

"You were always in such a hurry, dear, pastry needs time and patience, not whisking around and bashing flat as fast as you can manage."

The conversation stalled as they drank the tea, although Robin gave her mother credit for keeping going the longest. As soon as she felt it was no longer impolite, she made a move to go. Her mother was chattering on about the joys of a family Christmas. Robin wanted to be out before the thorny question of just who she would be likely to bring to such an event arose. But she was too late.

"It would be so nice to have four around the table instead of just the two of us, dear, but I suppose you've got other plans by now."

"It wouldn't be quite what you want though, would it, Mum? You know it would be a woman I'd bring home, and you made it quite clear how you felt about that long ago." Robin cursed inwardly; this was just what she'd wanted to avoid and now she'd opened it all up herself.

Her father spoke gruffly. "If you could trust us enough to bring your woman home, Robin, you'd find we never really meant that."

"That's true, dear." Her mother continued eagerly. "So does that mean there is someone, Robin dear? I'm so glad for you."

Once again a rush of emotion caused Robin to speak before thinking. "No, there isn't, Mum. I was daft enough to drive her away." She stopped abruptly, as much to prevent herself from pursuing this line of thought as from the knowledge that more would be inappropriate. "Well. Thanks for the tea and mince pie, Mum. It's been good to see you both again, but I'd better dash. Got a heap of things to do." She moved towards the door.

Her father stood too and there was another awkward pause as she faced her parents. "Don't leave it so long next time, will you Robin? We'd like to see more of our only daughter, you know, and your friends." He patted her shoulder briefly, before moving away. Robin's mother repeated the same request as they walked to the door.

"It's all a bit strange, Mum. I can't quite adjust to it. It's been so long, and I thought. ..." She swallowed hard and left the sentence unfinished. Her mother pecked her cheek quickly.

"I know, dear. Take your time. We're always here. Just don't take too long."

Driving away from the house Robin thought back. It was true that she bumped into her mother in town now and then, although not if she'd seen her first; and that her mother rang her quite regularly, but, as soon as she ascertained there was no crisis, Robin had quickly ended each call. Perhaps she should not have been quite so abrupt.

35

Penn made her way to the information desk in the centre of the library. "Do you keep old newspapers on file?" she asked the man behind the counter. "I'm looking for about eight or ten years ago. The national dailies."

She was directed to a room at the top of the building where the papers were stored on microfiche. It took her about half an hour to find what she was looking for. She read steadily, eyes squinting slightly against the blue of the microfiche slide.

Robin's life had certainly been splashed all over the papers, just as she'd said. Not just in a low circulation lesbian sports magazine. This was the real thing. Half the country would have read about women's football being a hotbed of lesbian activity, and been left with the impression that Robin was the central figure in every liaison.

Penn wondered how 'out' Robin was when this blew up in her face. Thinking about Robin's reserve, her need for privacy, she understood it better now. She recalled the night they first made love. There'd been a conversation in the bar that evening which had upset Robin. What had it been about? She wrinkled her brow in an effort to remember. That was it, the issue of 'outing' people against their will. She was sure now that Robin could not have been 'out' when the newspaper story broke.

Penn looked again at the byline to the article, Lucy Chappell. It was a well-known name and after a moment's hesitation she knew why. The woman was a columnist in one of the Sunday papers, mainly gossip stuff. She was a regular on radio and television quiz shows as well. Penn stored the information away. She put the microfiche files back on the shelf and made her way down to the ground floor. Glancing out of the window she saw the cold December drizzle and shivered. Maybe if she gave it another half hour it would ease off. She wandered over to the second-hand bookshop located to one side of the entrance. As she walked in, a photograph caught her eye and her pace quickened. She was right, it was one of the first women players at Deepdale Town.

On the bus, looking out at the persistent rain that darkened the already blackened buildings, Penn's thoughts drifted back. She'd felt secure in the warmth and concern that emanated from Robin that day on the beach. She didn't want to admit it at first. It unsettled her. She was over that, wasn't she? It was past, done with. She and Robin had moved on. They were friends now, that was all. There was no going back. This chain of thought came to an unhappy conclusion. She wanted to go back. She wanted to experience more than Robin's friendship again. For her, it wasn't over at all. Confronting this reality, Penn wondered, *"Just what am I going to do about it, that's the question? If there is anything I can do."*

36

Friday was one of those magically sharp, clear days that make winter bearable. The sun shone in a pastel blue sky, breath hung in the air, surrounding each head like a halo and frost picked out the minutest detail on every tree and blade of grass.

The evening before, looking out on the continuing drizzle, Robin had wondered if a walk would be worth the effort. She'd just get soaked to the skin. Now, she stood at the open back door, breathing the crisp cold air. Today was perfect. She knew exactly where to go. There was a long ridge walk with spectacular views she hadn't done for quite a while.

She gathered her map, waterproofs just in case, a bar of chocolate and a flask of hot, sweet coffee. Stowing them all in her small, well-worn backpack, she was about to go out the door when the phone rang. She answered in a slightly irritated tone.

"Hello? Oh, Penn, it's you. What's up?"

Penn's voice was a little hesitant. "Hi, Coach. I wondered if you have any time today, only ... there's something I want to show you. To do with this thing in *OUTfield*."

"I was just going out for the day, Penn."

"Oh. Sorry. Never mind. I'll catch you another time, then." Penn sounded disappointed and Robin made a snap decision.

"Look. I'm going into the dales for a walk. I'm passing your way. What say I pick you up? Could you be ready in about an hour?"

"Are you sure? I don't want to butt in."

"Of course. You'll enjoy it. It's a glorious day."

A couple of hours later, they were striding along a ridge with what seemed like the whole of Lancashire laid out below them in the sunshine. With a little extra effort, Robin thought, she could make out the sea sparkling in the distance. The nearer landscape was a mixture of brown ploughed fields, black hedgerows and green pasture, still silvered with frost. She breathed deeply, wondering why it was she didn't make the effort to get into the hills more often. It was so relaxing and invigorating at the same time. She moved along briskly, deep in her own thoughts, hardly aware of Penn keeping pace beside her.

Eventually, reaching an old circular stone sheep pen, Robin drew to a halt. She sat on one of the wide flat stones and leant back against the wall from which it had fallen. "Fancy some hot coffee?" She passed Penn a steaming mug. "So. What was it you wanted to show me?"

Penn rummaged in her pack. She handed Robin the December issue of *OUTfield*. "Look at page ten."

At the top of the page, outlined thickly by a black box was an apology statement. Robin read quickly. 'The editor apologises for the serious error made in the previous issue in printing an article about Penn Millard. She was misled by the reporter concerned. The impression given in the article is entirely erroneous. The magazine retracts every word, unreservedly. Penn Millard is a talented and professional sportswoman and *OUTfield* wishes her a long and successful career.'

Robin looked over at Penn in admiration. "Wow!"

Penn beamed. "Good isn't it? I got the name of the journalist from Cath and I went in to see the editor. Turned out she'd been absent when the story was approved. She'd already had words with the woman and the sub-editor. I thought there'd be a line or two in a corner."

"I'm impressed, Penn, truly I am."

"Well, it was thanks to you I did it." Penn, seeing Robin's raised eyebrow, went on hurriedly. "You believed in me. That was really important. I thought about what you said, about people forgetting and all that. You're right, but I wanted the record set straight. You said you'd written a letter, so I thought why not go in to see the editor? I can sort the football side out, like you said, but I didn't want Cath to get away with those lies. You can't just let people go on with that sort of thing and not try and stop them, can you?"

Robin was astounded. "I could have done with some of your wisdom years ago." She realised she'd spoken rather than thought the words and felt a little colour come up under her cheeks. "But most of what Lucy wrote about me was true."

"It was not!"

Robin looked up, her face twisted into a sardonic grin. "How would you know, Penn? You were still at school when it happened."

It was Penn's turn to blush. "I went to the library the other day and looked it up," she admitted, adding more insistently, "It might have been true about lesbians and football, but it made out you were involved with everyone. I don't see that being true. It was just as full of innuendo as the one last month about me."

Robin made a non-committal sound. After a moment, Penn spoke again, more quietly. "I'm not surprised you didn't do anything about it, Coach. It wasn't just in a lesbian sports rag, after all. It was the national dailies. And you weren't 'out' at the time were you? There's no comparison really."

"It was that I couldn't cope with." Robin's voice was low. "Not even my family knew I was lesbian. It devastated my parents, just blew us all apart."

"Mmmm." Penn watched her, feeling the pain Robin obviously still felt, as if it were her own. "That must have been awful. Far worse than what happened to me."

Robin raised her head. "But you dealt with it, Penn. It takes courage to confront these things. I just ran away." She glanced at Penn and then away. "You know, I'm really only sorting it out now, after all these years." Robin shook her head wearily. "I saw my parents the other day. Hadn't been for ages. I avoided them, thought they hated me. They don't, of course. It's pathetic really."

"It takes time to heal really deep wounds," Penn said. "Betrayal *is* painful. We all react to it in different ways. It's not pathetic to feel hurt."

Her words fell into an awkward silence. It was Robin, the more practised in the art of avoidance, who found an escape route, saying with a grin, "You seem to have an answer for everything, Penn. You should offer your services to *OUTfield* as an agony aunt. That way you'd get some financial compensation too." She shook the dregs out of the coffee mugs and stood up. "We'd better head back or it'll be dark before we get to the car, and it's quite a drive home."

37

The Christmas party in the bar was always on the Saturday of the weekend before Christmas itself. This year it fell on the twenty second. It was usually a lively occasion and tonight was no exception to the rule. Robin had hardly stopped since six and it was now ten o'clock. There were still people arriving, squeezing into the overcrowded room. Everyone was trying to catch up with everyone else. This annual event involved the whole of the Deepdale lesbian community and most of Burnden's as well.

It was the one night of the year when they hired temporary staff. That way, she, Sally and Ingrid could enjoy the party too. Even so, Robin always kept a weather eye on the proceedings. Once or twice she'd had to intervene to keep the peace between thirsty customers and rushing bar staff. One year, she'd caught one of the women stealing. Tonight, however, all was going well and the women were handling the never-ending orders with calm efficiency. Robin made a mental note to give them a good bonus.

The music was excellent; the DJ judging the mood and tastes of the crowd with flair and keeping the dance floor as crowded as the rest of the bar. The atmosphere was fizzing, sparkling with excitement, but there was a real warmth and sense of inclusion too. No one was being left out; friends or strangers, tonight everyone was welcome to the feast.

Robin moved through the crowd of women, pausing frequently to chat, her face showing the pleasure she felt at each renewed friendship. Gradually she gravitated to one corner, tucked in between the dance floor and where the pool table usually stood. Here were all the women with connections to football, and it was here Robin felt most at home.

Almost all the faces were known to her. Several of the Town players were there: Josie, Phil and Chris, Mandy. Phil was now quite obviously pregnant and blooming with it, her dark skin glowing with health. The morning sickness must be well and truly over, Robin thought. Then there were Burnden players, along with Jude of course, Penn among them. Older women, no longer active players, mingled with the rising young talent.

When the DJ began a series of Tina Turner numbers with "Simply the Best", the whole group moved onto the dance floor in one body. They never missed the chance to dance to Tina's music. They danced as a group, without specific pairings, turning and twisting, mixing and matching as the mood took them. Robin partnered Jude, Chris and Mandy before finding herself opposite Penn. She felt a thrill of pleasure as the two of them moved rhythmically together. Without any calculated effort, they remained paired even as the others interchanged around them.

The music changed to a slower tempo. Joni Mitchell's haunting voice filled the room with "A Case of You". Robin and Penn were still dancing. With the change in pace they moved smoothly into one another's arms, still keeping time.

The song was one of Robin's all-time favourites. Unthinkingly she hummed along, her mouth beside Penn's ear. Penn's skin prickled as she heard Robin sing the words, "you are in my blood, you're like holy wine". She became acutely aware of Robin's physical closeness, the way her arms felt crossed lightly behind her own back, the ripple of muscle in her thighs as they swayed to the beat. Her heart beat faster. Afraid to break the spell, she hardly breathed. The song ended and the music slid without pause into another smoochy number, "Move Closer".

Another couple of minutes passed and the song was drawing to a close before Penn dared to lift her head from Robin's shoulder. Their eyes met in a long look. Robin held Penn closer for the briefest of moments, then let her hands fall to her sides. "Drink?" Penn nodded and they wove through the crowds to the bar.

Each with a glass in hand, they found themselves a quieter corner and sat down. The intimacy of the moment on the dance floor retreated. The talk drifted round to plans for Christmas. Robin asked how Penn's family problems were going. Would she be able to go to her mum's for Christmas?

"No." Penn shook her head. "Things are a lot better between us now, but I still haven't managed to talk to her about any of it. Still, we get on better and to tell the truth I don't want to spoil that. He'll be there for Christmas so I decided against it. I'm staying at the flat."

"What about Flic and Janet, are they around too?"

Again Penn's response was in the negative. Robin's heart brought out her next words before her head could judge or censor them. "I'm stuck for company too. D'you fancy coming over on Christmas Eve? We could cobble something together in the way of a celebration, I'm sure."

There was another exchange of looks before Penn agreed. Almost in reaction, they both became animated again, moving out from their corner and rejoining the crowd. The rest of the evening passed quickly. Penn left about one in the morning, taking the chance of a lift with a group returning to Burnden. "See you about four, on Monday," Robin called as they said more general goodbyes.

38

Penn took great care with her choice of clothes on Monday afternoon. She wanted to look good, but at the same time, she didn't want to overdo it. Casual but intimate was the look she was searching for. In the end she chose a pair of soft cream linen trousers and a flannel overshirt, the blue of which picked out the colour of her eyes perfectly. A twisted leather belt fastened loosely at her hips emphasised the flatness of her stomach. An opal pendant necklace was her only other adornment, glittering in the opening of her shirt.

When Robin opened the door, Penn knew she had judged it right. Robin was in dark green pleated trousers and a deep red silk shirt with a patterned waistcoat over it. She too had spent a long time deciding what to wear. So far, so good. They almost heard the phrase pass between them.

Penn followed Robin through to the kitchen, noting the signs of her hasty efforts to tidy and clean. Robin succeeded in minimising their awkwardness with a dinner that needed preparing. It gave them something to do, preparing the meat, peeling and chopping vegetables, mixing ingredients for the pudding. They worked well together, slipping back into old habits of sharing.

In the sitting room, Robin reached down into the corner behind one of the chairs, pulling out a square parcel and handed it to Penn. "I came across this a while ago and it made me think of you."

Penn took the present and undid its wrapping, taking care with the paper. It was a book about the lives of stuntwomen from the early nineteen fifties to the present day. She turned the pages eagerly, recognising scenes from some of her favourite movies. "It's great. Thank you." She jumped up, remembering her own gift for Robin. "I got you something too."

She lifted a flat, thin packet from her bag and passed it to Robin, whose face lit up with excitement, like a child at a sweet counter. Robin ripped at the paper eagerly, a total contrast to Penn's careful removal. The contents fell out onto her lap. She turned over each black and white photograph reverently.

"Where on earth did you find these, Penn? They're wonderful." Her eyes shone as she studied the prints. "Here's Jo Gallagher, and Mary Price, and isn't this Sue Downes? They're all here, the whole team! Penn, you're a miracle."

Penn laughed with delight. She'd known the minute she saw the set in the second-hand shop at the library that Robin would love them. It was the original Deepdale Town women's team from the early nineteen twenties. She joined Robin in her study of the pictures, listening to and sharing the stories of who they were, the way they played, of 'history in the making' as Robin described it. The rest of the afternoon flew by.

The delicious aroma floating out of the kitchen alerted them to the time. They hardly paused for breath as they carried out the last-minute preparations and set the table together. The food was served, the wine bottle opened, and still they talked. They moved on from football, although it remained a recurring theme, into other sports, discussing the gold medal possibilities in the upcoming Olympic Games. Penn, catching sight of her new book, was reminded of a spectacular scene in a recent film she'd been to, describing it in graphic detail from which Robin recoiled in mock horror.

More seriously, they discussed the implications of a new private members' bill to rationalise the way in which television revenue to football was split between all clubs and players. "It'll be good for the professional players, no doubt about that," said Penn, "but I'm not sure about how it's going to affect the amateur game. And it still doesn't acknowledge that we're as popular as the men. The crowds are as big for a United game as they are for most first division men's games, you know."

"We're doing very well," Robin agreed. "If we can just get the fixture list better arranged to fill the full year. Have you heard any more about extending the top twelve, Penn?" This plunged them into a heated discussion of the relative merits of competing plans to extend the professional league.

The meal over, they cleared away, made coffee and talked. It wasn't until Robin brought out the Drambuie, that the tempo slowed a little and the conversation settled on the morals of journalists.

"They're like vultures, Penn, hovering round waiting for a disaster to happen just so they can feed on it. In fact they're worse; they create their own disasters to feed off when there aren't enough to go round."

"But not all of them," Penn disagreed. "A lot of them deal in serious news and analysis, not personal gossip. You can't tar them all with the same brush."

"OK, I'll give you that, but as for the rest of them .... I'm all in favour of a privacy law. They shouldn't just be able to poke their way into anyone's life. Some things are private."

"I agree it's a difficult line to draw, and a lot of mistakes get made."

"You mean a lot of people get hurt and their lives ruined," Robin finished for her.

"No," Penn smiled but made her own point. "I mean that it's a difficult line to draw but there is some justification for their interference, as you call it. It's one of the reasons for having the press, to investigate what goes on under the surface. Without the threat of exposure, there'd be a lot more corruption and malpractice."

Robin had to concede the point. "But it's the way they do it, Penn.

They're so unscrupulous. They lie and cheat to get the information, then come over all holier-than-thou when someone questions them. They trade in betrayal."

"But they can be taken in, too," Penn replied. "It was Cath who betrayed me, if you want to call it that. She just used a contact in the press. The journalist was only guilty of not checking her story properly."

"Maybe so, but I still say they trade in betrayal." Robin's jaw was set and a scowl settled on her forehead.

"It's because of that Lucy, isn't it? I can see she did you a lot of damage, but how did she betray you? Someone must have given her the facts." Penn's voice was serious but still a little puzzled.

"I gave her the information. We were lovers. Then she twisted it round, embellished a little for good measure, wrote it down for the world and his wife to read and walked out of my life leaving me to pick up the pieces. I'm still finding them."

"Shit," Penn whistled softly under her breath. "What a cow. Didn't you have any idea?"

"That she was going to do that? None at all," Robin said bitterly. "First I knew was a hysterical phone call from my mother. It was only afterwards that I realised what Lucy'd meant when she said she was going to make it, whatever the cost. And who was going to pay."

"Shit," repeated Penn, trying to understand the devastation there must have been. No wonder Robin had a strong liking for privacy. "I didn't have to deal with a personal disaster like that, Coach. It wasn't anyone I cared about who spilled the beans. And my sexuality wasn't exactly blown apart either, given that anyone reading OUTfield would be sympathetic to that anyway."

"You still seem to have dealt with it far better than I did."

"But there was less to deal with," Penn insisted. "Of course it's taken you a long time."

"Betrayal is painful whenever it happens. There's no excuse for it." Robin got up to retrieve the Drambuie bottle, replenishing both their glasses and setting it down nearby. They sat for a while in silence. Penn changed the music on the CD player, choosing some medieval choral singing as an unobtrusive background. The pure, soaring voices filled the room. As she walked back in front of Robin her hand was caught and held. She looked down into Robin's upturned face, disconcerted to see the anguish in her grey eyes. She squatted down beside Robin. "What is it?"

"I betrayed you, Penn. There was no excuse for that either." Her voice was hoarse.

"Hurt me, yes, but how do you mean betrayed?" Penn said softly.

"It's a long story. It goes back to the business with Lucy. I told you I was still finding the pieces, didn't I?"

"I've got plenty of time."

"I don't know how to start, really. I treated you like shit. I'm really sorry. I'd like to try and explain, not to excuse it, there is no excuse, I just need to tell you."

Penn settled more comfortably onto the floor at Robin's feet. "You did treat me pretty badly," she concurred. "I couldn't work out what I'd done to deserve it."

Robin's hand strayed into Penn's hair, pushing it back from her forehead. "You didn't deserve it, love. You deserved far better than I ever gave you. You brought me a joy and happiness I couldn't describe, and I threw it all right back in your beautiful face."

"Why?" The hurt was still strong in Penn's voice. "All I did was tell you I love you." She realised she used the present tense, but didn't change it, knowing it was still true. "And then the shutters came down and that was it."

Robin's distress increased. "Oh god, Penn. You didn't think it was that. It had nothing to do with what you said. I'm so sorry, Penn. I felt, I feel exactly the same. No, it's more complicated."

In the sudden quiet, Penn caught Robin's hand and pressed it to her lips. Robin's grip was tight in return. "Don't, love," she whispered. "Wait 'til I've told you everything, please." Penn nodded, eyes shining, but did not let go her hand.

Robin spoke again, haltingly and with many pauses. Penn's grip on her hand remained steady. "As I said, Lucy and I were lovers. She was the first woman I fell for, I was just twenty. I was truly passionate about her. I ate, breathed and talked Lucy. I was in love way over my head. Or at least that's what I thought it was. I thought she was too. We shared everything, Penn, and I mean everything. There wasn't a thing about my life she didn't know."

There was a long pause. "I gave ... I mean, she ... when we made love, well ... she knew me, Penn, physically she knew every inch of me. I held nothing back. I didn't know how, then." Robin's cheeks were flaming.

"It's OK. I understand." Penn's tone was gentle, warm and encouraging. "Go on."

"After she went it was like a part of me went numb. I clammed up. I always held back from people, never let myself get involved emotionally. Even with my closest friends, like Sally and Jude, who went through it all right beside me. There was always a bit of me I kept to myself, tucked away. And physically, well, I just never let any woman get that close again. I learned how to please them and distract them, but I knew I was cheating, especially with you. And then you touched me, entered me. ..." Robin stopped again. She took a deep swallow from the glass at her elbow, feeling the alcohol burn in her throat. She refilled the glass.

"That really rocked me, Penn. I didn't realise how deep I'd buried the hurt. I couldn't accept your love or my need for you, I just reacted blindly, shutting you out. I'm so sorry. I hated myself but I couldn't stop. It was torture to watch what I was doing to you."

"It was hard not knowing why. I went to sleep blissful and woke up to a nightmare." Penn spoke quietly.

"God, I'm so sorry, love. I was an absolute brute, unforgivable. But I was too tied up in myself to see it then. I loved you and it terrified me. I wanted to jump into bed and have you make love to me forever and I wanted to run a mile. I did run for miles that morning, while you were sleeping." She smiled ironically.

"I thought I'd made a huge mistake," Penn admitted. "I thought I misjudged your feelings really badly. There I was, thinking of lifelong commitment and you clammed up the minute I mentioned love. I couldn't see how I'd made such a fool of myself, how I could have got it so wrong."

"You didn't get that wrong at all. The mistakes were all mine." She put Penn's hand to her mouth. "How were you to know what a mixed-up mess I was? Believe me you didn't do anything wrong, Penn. As far as I'm concerned you never have and probably never will."

Robin drained her glass again. "Penn. If you want to go, you better go now. I want you to stay, but it's up to you."

"I want to stay too, but if I do, there'll be no holding back." Penn took Robin's face in her hands, cupping her palms around her cheeks, fingers reaching back into her hair behind the ears. Her eyes, direct and serious, were questioning. "I want all of you, Robin." She spoke her name for the first time. "I need you to be sure. Very, very sure."

"I am. I promise."

Robin reached out her hand to take Penn's as she got to her feet and led the way upstairs. The clothes, chosen so carefully only hours before, were discarded with hardly a glance. There was a moment of stillness as they took in each other's bodies, eyes searching out remembered freckles, curves and hollows. Robin let out an involuntary gasp. Penn held her arms open. There was an undercurrent of urgency in their caresses, but their movements were slow and sensual as they took their time with this rediscovery.

Finally they lay breathing deeply, bodies woven together, the sweat drying on their skin. Robin relished their powerful sexual smell. She felt replete, completely at ease, except for one small question teasing at her brain.

"Penn?" Robin's voice was drowsy.

"Mmmm." Penn nuzzled closer into her side, reluctant to let go of the lingering after-shocks of pleasure.

"Why have you never used my name before?"

Penn lifted her head slowly off the pillow to rest on her raised hand. With one finger she traced the line of Robin's jaw. "I don't know. Somehow "Coach" seemed to fit you best. There was always a distance between us, I s'pose. It was like I didn't have the right to it, too intimate." She grinned, "and you do like being in charge, Robin."

Other Onlywomen Press books

BEYOND THE PALE
Elana Dykewomon
0-906500-63-X
A story of Jews who fled violent anti-Semitism in Russia's Pale of Settlement to emigrate to New York's Lower East Side. Recreating events such as the Kishinev pogrom of 1903 and New York's Triangle Shirtwash Factory fire in 1912, the novel introduces Chava, her father (an orthodox rabbi), cousin Rose, midwife Gutke, and enigmatic Dovida who passes as a man. This moving chronicle spells out most of the 20th century's political passions – trade unions, anarchism, socialism, women's suffrage. Impeccable research aside, this is simply unforgettable fiction – vibrant, transgressive, heart-rending.

LOVE RUINS EVERYTHING
Karen X. Tulchinsky
0-906500-61-3
Nomi has been dumped by her girlfriend – for a man. After crying, brooding and plotting her revenge, she swears off love forever. But then, family relationships accompany Nomi home to the wedding of her widowed mother where conspiracy theories and gay (male) politics enlarge the plot – and love breaks out again. A tragicomic tale with gorgeous prose.

BULLDOZER RISING
Anna Livia
0-906500-27-3
A secret congress of old women plot to escape the death decreed for citizens over forty. This is the youth culture of the future. Superb, uproarious satire.

REBELLION
Jay Taverner
0-906500-58-3
Tumultuous adventure, historical romance and a lesbian coming-of-age story. The Lady Isabella and her maid servant, Hope, are girls of sixteen when the Jacobite rebellions begin in 1715.

MANY ARE CALLED
Pat Arrowsmith
0-906500-59-1
Set in 1950s Liverpool, this is the story of well meaning young Hilary who wants to be a Social Worker. Here she grapples with the intangible processes of casework and the frightening practicalities raised by 'problem families'. Touching fiction from a famous anti-war campaigner.

HATCHING STONES
Anna Wilson
0-906500-39-7
Mordantly witty novel that examines cloning as the means to male supremacy. The many gendered, multi-coloured populations of the Southern hemisphere are seen through the eyes of tall blond clones. And the women exiled to Antarctica develop other plans.

TOUGH AT THE TOP
Nicky Edwards
0-906500-45-1
Newly unemployed Felicity sets out to renovate a remote Norfolk cottage. The contemporary story frames another seen through the eyes of a neolithic lesbian whose spirit comments scathingly on Britain's modern times.

short story collections

A NOISE FROM THE WOODSHED
Mary Dorcey
0-906500-30-3
Winner of the 1990 Rooney Prize for Irish Literature.

SACCHARIN CYANIDE
Anna Livia
0-906500-35-4
Lyrical fantasy, speculative sci-fi, short thrillers and sexy fables.

STRANGER THAN FISH
J. E. Hardy
0-906500-32-X
Traditional families, heterosexuals on-the-turn and hard-won lesbian realities.

MOSAIC OF AIR
Cherry Potts
0-906500-44-3
From revamped fairy tales and Greek mythology through heady romance and gritty 20th century realism to satirical Sci-Fi. A collection that encourages the reader to see the world afresh.

poetry

BECAUSE OF INDIA
Suniti Namjoshi
0-906500-33-8
Prose essays plus verse selected from nine earlier collections.

THE HANG-GLIDER'S DAUGHTER: *New and Selected Poems*
Marilyn Hacker
0-906500-36-2

NOT FOR THE ACADEMY: *Lesbian Poets*
ed. Lilian Mohin
0-906500-60-5
Anthology of contemporary British and American verse. Poets include: U.A. Fanthorpe, Marilyn Hacker, Jackie Kay, Pat Winslow, Aleida Rodriguez, Judith Barrington, Minnie Bruce Pratt, Caroline Griffin, Maria Jastzebska, Maureen Seaton, Jane Miller, Joy Howard, J.P. Hollerith, Emma Greengrass, Jenny Factor, Ruth O'Callaghan, Pam Parker, Elana Dykewomon, Jewelle Gomez, Rosie Bailey, Naomi Replansky, Jan Sellers, Kate Foley.

ONE FOOT ON THE MOUNTAIN:
British Feminist Poetry 1969-1979
ed. Lilian Mohin
55 poets, contributors' notes and photos
0-906500-01-X

NOTHING WILL BE AS SWEET AS THE TASTE
Elana Dykewomon [also a novelist, literary editor]
0-906500-57-5

SOFT ENGINEERING
Kate Foley [first collection, award winning, mature poet]
0-906500-51-6

PASSION IS EVERYWHERE APPROPRIATE
Caroline Griffin [first collection; poet and dramatist]
0-906500-50-8

non-fiction

LEAVING THE LIFE: Lesbians, Ex-lesbians and the Heterosexual Imperative
Ann Menasche
0-906500-53-2
Analyses interviews with: bi-sexuals, never-het. lesbians, ex-lesbians, married (to men) lesbians and returnees (lesbian, straight and lesbian again).

FOR LESBIANS ONLY: a Separatist Anthology
ed. Sarah Hoagland and Julia Penelope
0-906500-28-1
Essays from more than 70 contributors document twenty years of activism and scholarship in the most blatantly lesbian campaigns of the 20th century.

AN INTIMACY OF EQUALS: Lesbian Feminist Ethics
ed. Lilian Mohin
0-906500-43-5
Anthology scrutinising lesbians' interactions with the mainstream in: traditional religion, psychology, sexual practice, disability politics, filmic representations. Rabbi Sheila Shulman, Dr. Celia Kitzinger, Dr. Rachel Perkins, Anna Livia, Patricia Duncker, Julia Penelope, Lis Whitelaw, Maud Sulter, Rosie Waite, Nett Hart, Joyce Cunningham.

CHANGING OUR MINDS: Lesbian Feminism and Psychology
Celia Kitzinger and Rachel Perkins
0-906500-47-8
Analysis of contemporary psychology and it's practical effects on lesbians. Amassing both American and UK research, Drs Perkins and Kitzinger present an anti-therapy argument.

VOLCANOES AND PEARL DIVERS: Lesbian Feminist Studies
ed: Suzanne Raitt
0-906500-48-6
Lesbian literary criticism anthology with essays by practitioners of the arts described as well as research stretching from the 17th through the 20th centuries.

crime novels/onlywomencrime

BURNING ISSUES
Meg Kelly
0-906500-56-7
In a run-down resort on the south coast, an elderly student dies a ghastly death and her tutor investigates. Neither local politics nor international criminals deter our vulnerable, lesbian protagonist from uncovering a ring of porn merchants to find the murderer.

FEARFUL SYMMETRY
Tash Fairbanks
0-906500-54-0
Older and fatter than most lesbian private detectives, Sam knows Brighton's gay communities. Amidst some misleading scandals involving religious fundamentalists, runaway teenagers and genetic engineering, she sets out to solve an especially tricky murder.

DIRTY WORK
Vivien Kelly
0-906500-55-9
Murder – or suicide – in a London hostel for the homeless. Our amateur sleuth isn't slowed down by steamy sex with a prime suspect or comfort from the police sergeant (an ex-lover). This is a witty, fast-paced mystery.

Onlywomen Press started in 1974. We publish books which question gender inequalities and heterosexual orthodoxies: poetry, literary and popular fiction, non-fiction. These are available from bookshops and libraries throughout Europe, Australia, Canada and the USA. Write to us for free mail-order catalogues.